THE AMATEUR GO

'I think they have to use the servants' entrance William,' said Lady Ulsborne lightly, and he flushed, and, seeing his annoyance, Catherine put in quietly:

'Mrs. Ravensbourne does not like noise because of disturbing Miss Edith, and so Amy and I go and come by the back stairs. It is the most sensible thing to do.' She held out her hand to her charge. 'Come along, dear. It is time we went.'

She took her off firmly, leaving William with a sense of frustration and a feeling of having been snubbed. He supposed he deserved it, after neglecting his daughter for so many years, but Miss Whittingham seemed uncommonly ready to put him in the wrong, and he did not like it. And yet there was a dignity about her and a pride in her dark eyes and pale face that convinced him that although he might not like her, she was the sort of young woman to whom he could safely trust Amy. She would impart to his daughter a sense of values and an integrity and honesty of purpose that had been unknown to the lovely, wayward creature who had stolen his senses and broken his heart....

**Also by the same author,
and available in Coronet Books:**

The Romantic Frenchman
Horatia
The Penniless Heiress
The Nursery Maid
The Apothecary's Daughter
A Parcel of Land

The Amateur Governess

Mary Ann Gibbs

CORONET BOOKS
Hodder and Stoughton

Copyright © Mary Ann Gibbs 1964

First published in Great Britain 1976 by Coronet Books

The characters and situations in this book are entirely imaginary and bear no relation to any real person or actual happening

This book is sold subject to the condition that it shall not, by way of trade or otherwise, be lent, re-sold, hired out or otherwise circulated without the publisher's prior consent in any form of binding or cover other than that in which this is published and without a similar condition including this condition being imposed on the subsequent purchaser.

Printed and bound in Great Britain
for Coronet Books,
Hodder & Stoughton, London,
by Hazell Watson & Viney Ltd,
Aylesbury, Bucks

ISBN 0 340 20508 3

1

Catherine Whittingham was dancing with Anthony Trantam when the Diamond Jubilee Year was born. They were waltzing to the strains of the 'Beautiful Blue Danube' and she had never been so happy in her life. Anthony was an excellent dancer, and his steps fitted themselves to hers as few others did: moreover that night she was more than a little in love with him.

'You ought always to wear that colour, Kate,' he said as they danced. Her dress was a shell-pink satin damask, with straps over the shoulders and the long, Princess line that was so fashionable that year: it made her look as slender and as graceful as a willow wand. It was the prettiest in her wardrobe, and with it she wore her mother's diamond necklace and a diamond clip in her dark hair. Her younger sister Bella, in the trailing white chiffon and pearls of a débutante, looked a child in comparison. Bella had large blue eyes, a pink and white complexion and fluffy fair hair, added to a helpless air that men were already finding irresistible.

General Whittingham was not in London with his daughters. The ball was being given by Anthony's mother, Lady Trantam, in their town house, for her youngest daughter Dulcie, who was Bella's contemporary and bosom friend, and the General had preferred to send his sister-in-law, Miss Abbott, with his daughters, to the select London hotel where they always stayed when they were in town. His dancing days were over and he remained at Grey Ladies to make the most of what hunting days were left before they went to Cannes for the spring.

Memories have a trick of clinging to trivial things, such as scents and sounds, and Catherine was never able to forget the scent of the hothouse flowers in that ballroom, nor the tune of the 'Beautiful Blue Danube' waltz. Whenever she was assailed by such scents afterwards, or the sound of the waltz, it would all come back to her: Lady Trantam's crowded ballroom, the dance band, the glittering chandeliers, the gay voices, her own pale pink dress and the look in Anthony's eyes as they danced out of the old life into a new one that was to be unlike any she had ever known.

As the clocks struck twelve and the old year died he stopped beside windows that opened on to a balcony and, thrusting them open with an impatient hand, swept her out into the crisp winter night to listen to the chimes that were ringing out over London.

'The Diamond Jubilee Year is beginning, Kate!' he said exultantly. 'The year that is to be the happiest of our lives, because you are going to marry me directly I come of age in May. In spite of your father's opposition, and the months that must still elapse before I'm twenty-five, I want your promise tonight, Kate . . . now, while we welcome the New Year in!'

She laughed up at him breathlessly, swept off her feet by his gay good looks, his assurance that she would say yes, by the feeling that she was in love, and then she glanced over her shoulder and among the dancers in the ballroom she saw Miss Abbott searching for her frantically, her face so grief-stricken and bewildered that instinctively she dropped her hand from Anthony's arm and went to her.

'Aunt Emily!' She took her aunt's hand. 'What is the matter? Are you feeling ill, dear? Come out on to the balcony and tell me what has happened!'

Miss Abbott allowed herself to be led on to the balcony and the cold air steadied her. She stared up piteously into her niece's face. 'It's your father, Catherine,' she said, and for the first time they saw the crumpled telegram that she was holding. 'He had an accident out riding this afternoon . . . the horse put his foot in a rabbit-hole and fell . . . rolling on him.'

'Oh no!' Catherine exclaimed in horror, the colour leaving her face, while Anthony drew closer to her side. 'Is he badly hurt?'

'Oh, Catherine!' Miss Abbott burst into tears. 'My darling, how I wish I hadn't got to tell you this . . . but he's dead, Kate . . . he's dead.'

And as she tried to take in the fact that she would never hear her father's voice again, behind her and around her all the bells of London clashed and clanged their riotous welcome to the Diamond Jubilee Year.

*   *   *

The old Queen had been on the throne for sixty years, and 1897 was the most brilliant and rewarding of them all. Every part of her Empire was to be represented in London that summer, from the Prime Ministers of the Colonies—Canada, Australia, New Zealand and South Africa—to princes from India, and soldiers from Sierra Leone and Borneo. They were bringing gifts too, though not all as magnificent as that of Cape Colony, which was to be a battleship of the first class, fit to take its place alongside the British Navy at Spithead.

General Whittingham, because of his distinguished services in India, was to have ridden in the procession immediately in front of the Indian contingent, and his daughters and their aunt had been promised places on one of the stands so that they would be able to see him clearly when he rode behind his Sovereign on June 22nd for the great Thanksgiving Service at St. Paul's.

But a rabbit-hole had altered everything, and when the Jubilee Year was only a few minutes old Catherine Whittingham had her world taken from her by the telegram that came to tell her of her father's death. Not that she was aware of the full extent of the catastrophe then: that was to come a week later, when, back at Grey Ladies on the day after the funeral, her father's lawyer, Mr. Jason, brought news of such a startling nature that, already stunned by the General's death, she could scarcely take it in.

It had been snowing hard all night, and after the carriage had taken him away to catch the afternoon train to London, she stood for a time in the library windows staring out at the undulating landscape beyond, now covered with white like the icing on a Christmas cake.

It was as hard to believe what the lawyer had told her as it was to realize that under all that white lay rose trees and wide borders and terraced gardens, joined overnight to the Broad Walk down to the lake, where the stone mermaids' heads stuck out from the frozen waste as if they had been buried alive and were calling for help. Catherine felt very much as if she were submerged in a frozen lake herself: she could neither feel nor think coherently.

Every year since she had been fifteen and Bella twelve General Whittingham had taken them to the South of France or to Italy from the beginning of February until Easter, and this year was to have been no exception.

He travelled in style, taking his carriages and servants, and Miss Abbott, who had lived with them since Mrs. Whittingham died, to act as chaperon. Every year villas were rented, music, language and drawing masters were engaged to instruct the two girls, while the General himself embarked on a social life which he felt to be fitting for one of his calling, looks and reputed wealth — a life in which, latterly, Catherine had taken part.

Their summers were passed at Grey Ladies, with the roses in bloom, and under the great trees that fringed the mown lawns the General and his daughters entertained their friends at croquet and lawn tennis, and long lazy afternoons of conversation. The long days and scented nights passed happily and contentedly — one might almost say idyllically — until September brought a round of visits to Brighton, or Cheltenham or Harrogate, to relieve the General's gout before the start of the hunting season. And if it had not been for the rabbit-hole life might have continued in this way for some years still, although, thought Catherine, numbed from Mr. Jason's visit, it could not have gone on much longer.

It appeared that her father had been living in a dream, refusing to face reality, and it seemed certain now that he had been using those visits abroad in an attempt at retrieving his dwindling fortunes at the gaming tables. She was still trying to find some excuse for him when old Grindall opened the library door and Anthony walked in.

'Anthony!' She went to him with a feeling of relief. 'How nice to have you home again!'

'I told you I would follow as soon as I could.' He took both her hands in his and held them closely. 'I've been waiting all the week for a message from you.'

'I have been so occupied . . . and then Mr. Jason came and has only just gone.' She saw him glance at Bella, who was fast asleep on a sofa in front of the fire, her golden hair brighter than ever in contrast with the deep mourning of her black dress, and with Glossy, her little dog, asleep on her lap. It emphasized the air of grief and desolation in the house that Glossy only raised his head to give the visitor an incurious glance before returning to his slumbers with a sigh.

Catherine took Anthony to the far end of the room, where they could talk in low voices without fear of disturbing her sister, while the dusk of the January afternoon crept over the snow outside. 'Mr. Jason has brought us terrible news,' she told him. 'Aunt Emily is too distracted to discuss it, and Bella is exhausted by crying, so that it is a relief for me to be able to unburden myself of at least a part of it to you. Perhaps if I can tell you something of our troubles they won't seem so bad, because you've always been a brother to me, Anthony.'

'It is not my fault that our relationship was not made a closer one long ago,' he reminded her. 'But we'll talk of that later. Tell me instead what has happened, and how I can help you.'

Her dark eyes met his courageously. 'Anthony, we are ruined. Father's fortune was never as large as we thought, and he has been living for years far beyond his income. The little that remains will be eaten up by debts, and even this house and its contents are no longer ours. The chair you are sitting on, and this table in front of me—everything except our own personal belongings—is the property of the bank. Grey Ladies will be sold up, and, melodramatic though it may sound, Bella and I will be thrown out on the world!' She managed a faint smile, but he saw her lips tremble in spite of her valiant efforts at control. 'That is the news that Mr. Jason brought us, so I suppose I cannot wonder that Aunt Emily has taken to her bed!'

'My poor Kate!' He was shocked and startled. 'Are you sure? Is nothing left?'

'Nothing.' She sighed deeply. 'It is Aunt Emily I'm most sorry for: I've got to break it to her that she can no longer live with us . . . she will have to go to Aunt Ellen in Putney.'

'But I thought you didn't like your uncle?'

'We don't, and neither does poor Aunt Emily. Father could not stand him, and quarrelled whenever they met. But at least he will provide her with a roof over her head and food to eat—which we cannot do.'

'Did Mr. Jason suggest how you and Bella were going to live?' Anthony's voice was heavy with sarcasm.

'Don't blame the little man, Anthony! It isn't his fault! Bella suggested we should go out as governesses, but he wouldn't hear of it.'

'I'm glad he showed that much sense!'

'You think it would be beneath our dignity?' She made a sad little grimace. 'We'd be a couple of very amateur governesses, I'm afraid, because Bella can't spell and I can't add up, though we can both play the piano and sing and speak French and Italian and we are experts at ballroom dancing! I suppose there *might* be some high-class finishing schools in a town like Brighton that would be glad of our services. Father once said Brighton had more schools to the acre than any other town in Britain!' She saw his expression and smiled sadly. 'Don't think me frivolous, Anthony! If I don't make a joke of it I shall cry ... and if I give way everything is lost!'

'I know.' His arm went round her shoulders. 'Kate, my darling, there is only one way out of this business. We won't wait until I come of age: we'll marry at once. It isn't my fault that my idiotic father made the stipulation that I was not to inherit until I was twenty-five. Just because he was wild in his youth he must look on me with a jaundiced eye! But if we get married now you and Bella can make your home at Trantam Court and the bank can do what it pleases with Grey Ladies. You will be safe, and I shall be the happiest chap on earth.'

Catherine drew a deep breath, suddenly near to the tears she had rejected. 'And your mother?' she reminded him unsteadily. 'What will she say to such a marriage for her beloved only son?'

'Mother has always been for it. You know she has! When I broached the subject to her last summer, and again just before our London ball, she said she would like to have you for a daughter-in-law better than any other girl in the world.'

'But I had prospects then ... I was a rich man's daughter. Circumstances have altered things so much that I doubt if she would extend the same warm welcome to me now ... And I'm too proud to catch at marriage—even with you, my dear!—as a means of support for myself and Bella.'

'That's pure nonsense. I love you and I'm pretty sure that you love me ... and, apart from that, what other life is open to a girl in your position but marriage?'

'I don't know, but I think I should try to find out. As a beginning I might advertise my services as a companion to a lady.'

He took his arm away roughly and got to his feet, his handsome face flushed with anger. 'You might as well become an amateur governess, Kate!'

'I think not. Small, unruly children would drive me mad, whereas Bella and I have been an old lady's companion for a good many years now and we have managed to be very happy.'

'But Miss Abbott isn't an old lady . . . at least, not all that old! You should see my Aunt Sarah in Brighton, who gets through her companions at the rate that Dulcie and Alice get through their hats. I guarantee if you were *her* companion for a week it would cure you of ambitions of that sort!'

Catherine was not convinced. 'Although if an old lady did take me as her companion,' she conceded unwillingly, 'I don't suppose she would take Bella as well.'

'Whereas Trantam Court will welcome you both with all the love and joy in the world! Say you'll have me, Kate . . . and as soon as possible.'

'Dear Anthony!' Her eyes were now unashamedly wet. 'The offer is a tempting one . . . I don't feel very independent or defiant this afternoon . . . and it's because of that that I can't answer you right away. You must talk it over with your mother first, and I'll promise you this: if she thinks the same way as you then maybe I will bring Bella with me to Trantam Court.'

'God bless you for that!' He wanted to snatch her up in his arms and seal the bargain there and then, but the sadness in her face prevented him. A warning note had been struck between them, and he felt that she was still so shocked by her father's death and the lawyer's visit that she could not stand any more. He hurried home and found his mother writing letters in the little morning-room, and sat down by her fire and told her that he was going to marry Catherine.

'Well,' said Lady Trantam composedly, 'I rather thought you would, darling, when a decent time had elapsed after the General's death. I like a June wedding best . . . it is such a charming time of year.'

'But there's no time now to think about etiquette or a convenient time of the year, Mother.' He told her briefly about the state of the girls' finances. 'They are quite penniless. Everything is to be sold and they will have nowhere to go but here. So I told Kate she must marry me right away.'

Lady Trantam's pretty face was as calm as ever, and the dismay she felt was not visible: she had been brought up never to exhibit emotion. 'And what does dear Catherine say to that?' she asked.

'Oh, she is too bothered to know what she is saying . . . but I'm pretty sure she will have me in the end.'

'I should think any girl in that position would, dear!'

Anthony did not think he liked the implication of that remark. 'Mind you, I'm going to have a tussle with her,' he went on hastily. 'She started talking about being an old lady's companion or some such rubbish . . . Can you imagine Kate in such a position?'

'But I think she is wise not to be rushed into marriage before she has had time to think things out, all the same.' Lady Trantam sounded thoughtful. 'And not all old ladies are hard to get on with. I daresay your Aunt Sarah might be willing to have her for a time if one explained the circumstances.'

'Mother, Aunt Sarah is a terrible old woman! And how do you know that she needs a new companion?'

'Your Aunt Sarah *always* needs a new companion, darling. If she engaged one last week she would most certainly be needing another before the month is out. And at this time of year she will welcome a change, more particularly because most of her friends leave their houses to painters and decorators in March, and she gets so bored that she is glad of any diversion, as she never goes away herself. She might be flattered at the thought of having a General's daughter for a companion.'

'I would like to think she would pay her a large salary on that account, but, knowing Aunt Sarah, I'd say she would pay next to nothing. And in any case it is a waste of time to talk about it, because I'm going to marry Kate right away and settle her future and mine.'

'I still maintain that you should not rush the poor girl,' said his mother mildly. 'Let me write to Aunt Sarah, Anthony. She may offer to have both girls on a visit for a time, and we have to think of them, after all. It is going to be a terrible ordeal for them having to watch their home being sold up over their heads.'

After a good deal more on these lines she managed to persuade her son to abandon his first idea of an immediate marriage.

'But I shall insist on Kate being engaged to me,' he added. 'I shall not be happy until I have her promise.'

'You mustn't be selfish, darling. We have to think of poor Kate first,' said his mother serenely, and directly he left her she wrote another letter, which she marked urgent, and addressed to Mrs. Henry Trantam, Number Three, Mecklinburgh Square, Brighton.

I am at my wit's end to know what to do, she wrote. *Anthony is in love with a penniless girl, and if I cannot part them quickly I'm afraid he will rush into a marriage that we shall all regret.*

I like Catherine Whittingham, and I am devoted to her little sister Bella, who is Dulcie's great friend and much more pliable, but I have never been happy over Anthony's choice of Kate. The General was against it all along, and now of course we all know why — he wanted to get a much richer husband for his elder daughter than my poor boy! But apart from any question of money, Catherine is too self-willed and autocratic. She must have her own way, and Anthony thinks she can do no wrong, and I do feel that such a marriage would be disastrous for him. He needs a wife who will look up to him and admire him, not keep him on leading strings all the time. Entre nous I hear that General Whittingham has been criminally extravagant, and Catherine is very like him. There will be no stopping her once she is married to Anthony. He will do everything she tells him without question . . .

The answer to this letter was addressed to Miss Whittingham at Grey Ladies, and written in an old-fashioned hand on thick grey notepaper, with a black crest on the flap of the envelope.

In it Mrs. Henry Trantam said she had heard from Lady Trantam the details of their sad loss, and of the unfortunate pecuniary situation in which they had been left. She understood that it was in their minds to seek employment of some kind, and as her companion was under notice to leave at the end of March she would be prepared to take one of the Miss Whittinghams in her place. She had no objection to her sister accompanying her, and would board and lodge her for a time as long as she could make herself useful until she found suitable employment in Brighton.

The word 'employment', repeated twice, made Catherine wince, but Bella only laughed.

'Dulcie always said their Aunt Sarah was eccentric,' she said. 'But I daresay her bark is worse than her bite. It would be wonderful to see dear Brighton again: the air there is like wine.'

The situation as explained by Mr. Jason seemed to be desperate and Catherine felt she must make up her mind quickly. Miss Abbott came out of her prostration sufficiently to join the two girls downstairs, and while Bella was out walking with Glossy that afternoon Catherine gave her aunt Mrs. Trantam's letter to read and asked for her advice, which showed the state of her mind, because she had never asked her aunt's advice about anything in her life.

Miss Abbott did not like the tone of the letter and said so. 'She sounds a disagreeable and cantankerous old lady,' she said. 'And I can't see why you and Bella should do anything so . . . degrading . . . as try to earn a living for yourselves. It's not a thing you've been brought up to, and, after all, dear, your father was a very famous soldier. His grateful country owes something to his daughters, surely?'

'He had a pension, Aunt Em, which he commuted.'

'I know that, dear, but at the same time he had many influential friends, who would be delighted to do something for you two girls if they were asked. Nothing magnificent, perhaps . . . nobody would want to impose on them . . . but they might be persuaded, and happily persuaded too, to provide some small fund between them on which you could live quietly in a little house together. Even the dear Queen might help, if such a thing were to be brought to her notice in her Diamond Jubilee Year.'

Catherine ignored the dear Queen and asked if her aunt were suggesting that they should pass the hat round among their relatives and friends?

'Well, dear, that is rather a crude way of putting it, but I suppose it *is* what I meant.'

'Mr. Jason suggested the same thing to me when he was here.' Catherine got up and walked restlessly to the window: the snow had gone now, but there was a stretch of even purer white under the bare trees where the first of the snowdrops were coming through. 'I told him I could not accept charity from anybody as long as I had health and strength, but I am not so sure of Bella. She is not as strong as I am, and if Mrs. Trantam should engage me as her companion do you think Aunt Ellen would take her to live with her in Putney too?'

Miss Abbott shook her head. 'I am sure she wouldn't, my love. As far as I'm concerned Bella could share my last crust, but unfortunately the crusts in Putney will belong to your Uncle Josiah and he is not one to share them with anybody.'

'Then I shall have to think of some other plan for Bella. Don't worry, Aunt Em. I'll find something for her.' But although Catherine spoke cheerfully her heart sank at the thought of little Bella having to battle her way alone in an unkind world, and her spirits were not raised by reading Mrs. Henry Trantam's letter a second time. Anthony's old aunt did not appear to have much sympathy for other people's troubles.

But when Anthony came again to beg her to give up the whole project, and get engaged to him without any more delay, she discovered that her mind was made up. The fact that his mother had not added her persuasions to his, but had written off at speed to Mrs. Henry Trantam, seemed significant of a desire to be rid of her, and as she realized for the first time how cold her own world could be to those unwise enough to run into misfortune, she was hurt to the quick. If she had been deeply in love with Anthony she would have defied his mother's disapproval and the unkind gossip of their friends, but there was no 'Beautiful Blue Danube' waltz now to sway her senses, and in the cold light of day she had to face facts as she had never had to do before.

'If I didn't care so much for you, or if I cared more, I'd marry you,' she told him quickly. 'Our friendship makes it so much harder for me to say no. But I don't love you, and I'm too good a friend to want to ruin your life.'

'Suppose you let me decide what will ruin my life? But I'll let you go to Aunt Sarah for a few weeks, if you are set on it, while Grey Ladies comes under the hammer, because if anyone will make you change your mind about me it is that old woman in Brighton. She runs me down so often that with your propensity for defending the underdog you'll be forced to stick up for me, and you'll find yourself even getting to love me in the end.'

So Catherine wrote to accept Mrs. Trantam's offer, and as the bank was to take possession at Lady Day, the rest of their time was spent in packing away clothes they would not need, and a few personal treasures such as favourite books and the pictures, curtains and cushions from their own little sitting-room upstairs, which Anthony had promised to store for them at Trantam Court.

Dulcie was to look after Glossy until his mistress could have him with her again, and, after a tearful parting with her little dog and his new owner, one windy March morning Bella set out with her sister and Miss Abbott for the station.

The blackthorn was white in the hedges, and the countryside had acquired overnight a golden look as if spring were not so far away, after all, and as they drove through familiar and well-loved lanes for the last time Catherine felt a lump in her throat and a stinging at the back of her eyes.

She had refused to allow Anthony to see them off, saying that prolonged farewells were only a protraction of the agony:

the old life was finished and it was better to cut with it quickly and cleanly. Tears would not bring back one penny of the gold that their father had poured out so recklessly at the roulette tables abroad, and his elder daughter set her chin proudly and declared that they would do without it very well.

2

Mr. Jason met their train and conducted them across London in a cab, and after they had seen a dejected Miss Abbott off to Putney the lawyer purchased two first-class tickets to Brighton.

'But we can't afford such luxuries as first-class travel now!' protested Catherine. 'Dear Mr. Jason, we must begin to cut our garments according to our cloth.'

'You may do as you please later, Miss Whittingham,' he replied sadly. 'But allow me to send you on your way today in a style fitting to the General's daughters.' He hesitated. 'Am I right in supposing, Miss Whittingham, that you have no bank account?'

'You are, Mr. Jason.' The General had not believed in bank accounts for women.

'Then allow me to give you this.' He took a sealed envelope from his pocket and put it into her hand. 'There is a small sum of money there in bank-notes—not very much, I'm afraid, but it will serve you as a stand-by should things turn out not so well as you anticipate. It was lying idle, a small emolument of your father's, rescued from the estate. It will not keep the wolf from the door for long, but if the aforesaid wolf should venture unpleasantly near at any time in the future, may I beg you, my dear Miss Whittingham, to write to me at once, not as your father's lawyer, but as an old friend?'

Catherine thanked him and gave him the promise he asked, and he walked up the platform with them to find an empty compartment.

'I wish you had a maid with you,' he said anxiously. 'I don't like to see two young ladies travelling alone.'

'It's the first time that we haven't had our dear Parker to look after us,' said Bella tearfully. 'It nearly broke my heart to part with her, but she said she would refuse to take anything but a temporary post, in case we needed her.'

'We may *need* her,' said Catherine with a sigh, 'but I'm afraid we shall never be able to afford a personal maid again.'

They found a carriage and Mr. Jason saw them into it and their luggage into the guard's van, and had stepped back with his hat in his hand while the engine, with a puff of black smoke and a shriek from its whistle, was about to start, when a lady and gentleman hurried down the platform followed by the guard, and stopped at the door of their compartment.

'Here you are, my dear,' said the gentleman, as the guard wrenched open the door, and he almost lifted the lady into the carriage in his haste. 'Our friend here has held the train five minutes for you, and we can't ask him to delay it for another ten while you search for a carriage to suit you.' He climbed in after the lady, the guard shut the door on them and pocketed the gentleman's tip with a respectful touch of his cap, his green flag was waved, and Mr. Jason, looking ruffled and put out, was left behind on the platform.

The newcomers settled themselves in the far corners of the carriage, the man with some impatience and the lady with a pout of disgust because they could not travel alone.

'I had forgotten your propensity for being late for appointments, Helen,' said the gentleman. 'Otherwise I would have ordered the carriage half an hour earlier.'

'There is so much that one only remembers at the last moment,' she complained. 'And then Dick was not there, you see. He always remembers everything for me.'

'Then he should stop the habit, as it is very bad for you. You will have no memory left if everybody works so hard to save you from using it.'

Catherine and Bella exchanged glances of some amusement. The man was clean-shaven and dark, and would have been handsome if his expression had been less severe and his features less heavy, but there was an air of power about him, and a suggestion of latent force and authority that appealed to Catherine's independent spirit. She fancied he might be a man who would not stand being crossed or questioned and who was accustomed to having his own way.

The lady with him was a direct contrast: as fragile as he was strong, as fair as he was dark, as flutteringly feminine as he was all virile masculinity, and yet under her pouting playful manner Catherine guessed that she was equally used to getting her own way. She was conjecturing about the business that was bringing them to Brighton at that time of year when the lady began talking about a Mrs. Ravensbourne, and about a child called Amy for whom she professed a great deal of anxiety and for whom she was going to interview a governess in Brighton on the following day.

'I hope you are properly grateful for what I'm doing for you, Will,' she added playfully. 'It is most inconvenient for me to visit Brighton just now. My sister-in-law cannot have me longer than a couple of nights, as she is leaving for Paris on Saturday ... How I envy her! Paris is so wonderful in the spring!'

Her remarks were brushed aside with some impatience, her companion remarking that as he only saw Paris when he was there on business it could rain or snow as long as he found customers for his cloth. The lady rated him for his commercial mind.

'But I am a tradesman first of all, my dear,' he replied equably. 'And you could have saved yourself a great deal of inconvenience by not going to Brighton. There are other governesses to be had, I suppose.'

'But not like this one!' The lady dropped her voice and said something that Catherine did not catch, and he shrugged his shoulders indifferently.

'Amy looked well enough the last time I saw her,' he said, and added: 'She is not an attractive little girl: she scowls too much.'

'And no wonder she scowls!' cried his companion indignantly. 'I would too if I were in her shoes, poor mite. I know you think a great deal of your aunt, Will, but I wouldn't trust one of my darlings within miles of her if she hated them as she hates your poor little Amy!'

'My dear Helen, your geese have always been swans and your molehills mountains!' He was determined to laugh at her, and she was offended and took up a novel and began to read, but not for long, because she was not a person to be silent for more than a few minutes at a time. She soon put it down and asked if he had received a letter from Mademoiselle.

'Amy's French governess,' she explained, as he looked politely puzzled. 'The woman I found for her last summer and who left just after Christmas. Dick forwarded a letter from her to your address in Yorkshire a few days ago.'

'That explains why I have not received it, then, as I have not been to Yorkshire since I returned to England last week. But I daresay it will keep. It is probably only to tell me that I owe her some money.'

'No,' said the lady thoughtfully, 'I don't think it would be that.' She sent him a malicious little smile which escaped him: he was tired of the conversation, and catching Catherine's interested eyes on them at that moment he picked up his newspaper and began to read, replying to his companion's further attempts at conversation with such brevity that she gave it up and went back to her novel.

Catherine kept her eyes for her sister and the scenery outside the window for the rest of the journey.

*   *   *

Mecklinburgh Square was in fact an oblong with three sides of fine, dignified houses facing the sea and one another over an expanse of wind-swept gardens, all the houses there with one glaring exception painted a white that had mellowed with wind and spray.

The town with its shops and the cottages whose poverty was only matched by the slums of the big industrial cities, were safely hidden behind that wide, white sweep, and in front was the open sea. The houses possessed basements below and three or four storeys above, their windows were large, and on the drawing-room floor curved balconies were like a black lace insertion on creamy dresses.

Mrs. Henry Trantam's house had the advantage of a western aspect that included an almost unbroken view of the sea. Its area steps were as white as the shallower ones that led up to the green front door, and its windows shone as brightly as the brass knocker on the door, while behind the windows Swiss net curtains were draped softly over others of brocade and velvet.

But at Number Five next door the curtains hung as straight as lace curtains could, the windows were kept shut to avoid the unfriendly winds that swept across the square from the sea and there was not a leaf in its area, nor a stain on the iron railings which were washed down by the boy Albert twice a week. It was a house that stood out from the rest, being painted a dull brown, and its owner, the lady of the house, had been known to open the door herself to visitors still wearing the black alpaca apron and gloves that she put on every morning to dust her drawing-room.

Mrs. Henry Trantam's visitors averted their eyes from the house when they paid their calls, and their menservants turned outraged backs on it when tendering cards at Number Three in case they should catch sight of an alpaca apron and a pair of gloves where none should be. It was felt that though the owner of Number Five might keep her own carriage she was no lady.

But on the March afternoon when Mrs. Henry Trantam's carriage brought Catherine Whittingham and her sister to her door from the station the two girls were far too apprehensive of Anthony's formidable aunt to have noticed if her neighbour had been a chimney-sweep with the brush of his calling hanging outside.

The promise of fine weather had deserted them on the way down and it was now raining heavily, and as they waited for the front door to admit them they cast disappointed glances at the sea, colder and greyer and more uninviting than they had ever known it before.

'I wonder why it is,' said Catherine, 'that in looking back on happy days the sea is always blue and the sky the clear one of summer?'

'I wish Aunt Em were with us!' Bella's teeth were chattering in the cold wind that whistled up the square, but Catherine remembered that Miss Abbott had Bella's habit of wilting in a crisis and she felt she had enough on her hands at the moment.

The door was opened by a butler as benign and grey-haired as their own dear Grindall, and they were taken upstairs to the large drawing-room overlooking the square. Mrs. Trantam was waiting for them by a cheerfully blazing fire, and the girls were pleasantly surprised by her appearance. From Anthony's description they had expected to find a very old lady, but Mrs. Trantam was not much over sixty: there was scarcely a grey hair in the fringe that curled on her forehead, and no sign of a lace cap anywhere. Her eyes were a bright blue and very shrewd, and her dress, of a plum-coloured cloth, was obviously the work of an expert dressmaker, while the jewellery she wore was beautiful and well chosen.

Her manner was abrupt but kind, and she did not wait for them to come to her but got up and came to them, moving as quickly as she could, and it was only when they saw how she leaned on the stick in her hand that they realized she was lame.

'Did Anthony tell you?' she asked. 'Broke my leg out hunting years ago and been lame ever since.' She took Catherine's hand and subjected her to a keen scrutiny. 'You are Miss Whittingham. I recognize you from Lady Trantam's description . . . And *you*,' she went on, turning to Bella, 'are the younger one . . . the delicate one!' Sudden warmth sweetened her welcoming smile. 'Bella, she called you. May I guess that your name is a somewhat longer one?'

'It is Isabella, Mrs. Trantam.' Bella smiled back timidly, showing her dimples, and Mrs. Trantam did not leave go of her hand but held it more closely as she drew her towards the fire.

'Then I will call you Isabella if I may, my dear, because I detest shortened names. If a man is christened William why must he be called Willie? So far less dignified! And Isabella is much prettier than Bella! I'm sorry that Brighton has given you such a poor welcome, but I told my housekeeper to see that there were good fires everywhere to make up for it. Your hands are like ice, child . . . Come and sit down and warm yourself before you see your room. I am sure you must be frozen after such a long journey. Were the carriages heated, or did you have foot-warmers?'

'There were hot-pipes in the carriages all the way.'

'I'm glad to hear it. March is a sad, treacherous month, with a chilling smile, and one's feet can become like stones in a railway carriage. A travelling rug is not nearly enough to keep out the draughts. I hope you had a luncheon basket?'

'Yes, we did, on our way to London. Our lawyer, Mr. Jason, insisted on it.'

'It's a good thing he did, even if he does not appear to have looked after your interests very well in other directions.' Mrs. Trantam made Bella sit on a chair beside her own by the fire, leaving Catherine to find a seat where she chose, which she did with a wry little smile.

But realizing that this was a foretaste of what the lot of a paid companion must be, and the sooner she got used to it the better, she was pleased to see how taken Mrs. Trantam was with Bella. And who could help it? she thought affectionately. Her sister looked lovely in the black coat and hat: the depth of the mourning emphasized the bright gold of her hair and the wild rose colour in her cheeks, while it did nothing at all for the elder Miss Whittingham except to put ten years on to her age.

Throughout that first afternoon and evening no mention was made of their future employment: they were treated as guests, and moreover as the General's daughters, rather than as a paid companion and her younger sister, both dependent on the whims of their temporary hostess.

Catherine's room was a small one at the back, but she was glad to find that Bella had been given a large airy apartment with a window overlooking the square, and also that Mrs. Trantam's maid, Hannah, had unpacked for her sister. She left her own unpacking until the next day, taking from her box only the things she would need for the night, and at seven o'clock on the following morning she was awakened by a housemaid with a small pot of tea, a few slices of thin bread and butter and a large brass can of hot water.

'Please, miss, the mistress hopes you slept well, and she will be obliged if you will see her alone in the morning-room directly after prayers,' said the girl, as she packed towels round the can in the large china basin on the washstand to keep it hot. She added that prayers were at half past eight and breakfast was in the breakfast-room directly afterwards.

'But is your mistress down by half-past eight?' asked Catherine. At Grey Ladies they had favoured later hours for rising.

'Down? Why, lor' bless you, miss, she is often up and dressed by half-past six on a summer morning and walking in the square before breakfast!'

In spite of her lameness Mrs. Henry Trantam appeared to be no weakling, and Catherine dressed quickly and went to her sister's room, to find her ready and stationed at the window looking at something that interested her in the gardens of the square.

Catherine joined her: the sun was shining and in the early light the sea had shed a lot of the greyness of the day before, and, although the waves still showed a yellowish tinge, the water between was green, and the sun flashed on their curling crests and turned the wings of the seagulls above them to glistening white. But Bella was not watching the sea or the empty parade, and as Catherine entered the room she spoke without turning her head.

'Look, Kate!' she said. 'Come and look at that little girl down there in the gardens with her mother . . . at least, I'm not sure that she *is* her mother: the child looks too shabby to be the daughter of so fine a lady! But come over here and tell me if you don't recognize one of them.'

She drew the curtain aside and Catherine saw a child with

chestnut hair flying over her shoulders under a battered straw hat, the ugly brown of a shabby coat that was too small for her dark against the emerald-green that was pushing up into the dead winter grass in the gardens, and beside her, smiling down at her, a slender, fashionably dressed woman.

'Why,' Catherine said in surprise, 'that is the lady we travelled down from London with yesterday! I'd recognize those sables anywhere! Which house do they come from?'

'I think there's a carriage waiting for them,' said Bella. 'It has turned the corner of the square, so you can't see it for a moment, but a groom has been walking the horses up and down for some time.'

As she spoke they saw the child's companion look at a watch that was pinned by a brooch to the lapel of her coat under the sables: she said something and held out her hand, and the little girl took it and drew it round her neck. Thus closely knit, they turned and walked back slowly over the grass until they came across the road to the house next door to Mrs. Trantam's. Here they paused, waiting for the carriage to come back and stop beside them, and then the lady stooped and embraced the little girl lovingly, and stood on the pavement and watched her as, with a kind of shrinking reluctance, she mounted the steps of Number Five.

Somebody else had evidently been waiting for her morning walk to end, because the front door opened at once and swallowed her up as if it were the mouth of a dragon and she a dainty morsel in a fairy-tale. The lady stood where she was for some moments after the door had closed, and then she stepped into the carriage and was driven away.

'Now isn't that queer?' said Bella. 'To come here alone to see that funny little girl at this time of day, and then to drive off without even going inside the house with her! ... Do you think she can be the child's mother, because, if she is, why isn't her husband with her?'

'My dear, romantic Bella,' said Catherine, smiling, 'I should say it is their business and not ours!'

'No, but you must admit that it looks very queer,' persisted her younger sister. 'I didn't like the look of that vulgar man in the railway carriage yesterday. Didn't you hear him saying that he was a tradesman ... almost boasting of it, as if it were a thing to be proud of! It was quite dreadful to think that he was the husband of such a charming person.'

'What made you think he was the lady's husband?'

'Oh, but I'm sure he was . . . I heard her talking about a little girl called Amy and how she was coming to Brighton to find a governess for her. I think she had been married before, you know, and the little girl next door is her child by her first husband. She has to keep her there—with an old servant, I daresay—because her cruel step-father hates her and won't let his wife see her except by stealth.'

'Oh, Bella, what a vivid imagination you have!' Catherine couldn't help laughing at the story her sister had woven round the pair. 'Have you decided how the first husband died?'

'No, but perhaps he was drowned at sea, or killed in a skirmish on the North West Frontier in India. He may have been in the Army there.'

'Or he might have been a city alderman who died from eating a surfeit of oysters at the Lord Mayor's Banquet!'

'It's all very well to laugh at me, Kate, but what explanation have you got for what we have seen?'

'From what I overheard in the railway carriage,' said Catherine, 'it was the gentleman's little girl for whom the lady was to engage a governess. I don't know why he could not do it himself, but perhaps the lady is a close relative—they called each other by their Christian names—and she may have wished to save him the trouble. This may be the little girl in question, though—I grant you that.'

'Isn't it strange then that she should be living next door to us here?'

'Quite a coincidence.' Catherine smiled affectionately at her sister. 'And now come away from the window and tell me how you slept in that comfortable bed?'

'Very badly,' said Bella discontentedly. 'I kept wondering if Mrs. Trantam was really as nice as she seemed to be—Dulcie said she was such a terror—but she was so kind and considerate that I felt she might not be so bad after all. And then I kept waking up in the night and thinking that perhaps today she'd show herself in her true colours and send us packing.'

'Indigestion,' said Catherine. 'The chicken in the luncheon basket was remarkably tough.'

'Well, whatever it was, the more I thought about it the more frightened I became, because we've nowhere else to go, have we? What will we do, Catherine, if we can't stay here?'

Catherine kissed her and laughed at her fears.

'I never met anyone like you, Bella! If there isn't anything to worry about you'll spend a whole night fancying there might be! Mrs. Trantam isn't an ogre, and if she should change her mind about employing me, why, Brighton is full of lodging houses and girls' schools, and we shall be able to live in the one and earn our bread-and-butter by teaching in the other. There is a hundred pounds in that envelope that Mr. Jason gave me yesterday, and if that isn't enough to keep us from starving there's Mother's jewellery—my diamonds and your pearls that we can sell. So trust me, darling, and don't worry over anything.'

Bella smiled uncertainly, but she looked reassured.

'I don't know what I'd do without you, Kate,' she said. 'I don't know why I worry about things when you never worry at all. I expect it's the way I'm made.'

'Well, then, let me pin your hair more neatly at the back, and then we'll go downstairs.'

'I shall never be able to do my own hair properly. I don't know how you can do yours so well, Kate. You look just as if our dear Parker was with us still.'

'You'll soon learn, darling. It's only a matter of practice.'

'Well, I don't like it,' said Bella plaintively. 'I'd much rather have Parker help me to dress and do my hair. It's horrible being poor. Some of my ball-dresses have hooks and eyes all the way up the back. How am I going to do those up without help?'

Catherine forebore to remark that it was unlikely she would find many opportunities for wearing the dresses in question, and led the way downstairs.

Mrs. Trantam was already in her place behind the writing-table in the morning-room, a large bible open in front of her and a pair of gold pince-nez perched on her nose. The servants were assembled, and as the two girls arrived their hostess greeted them with a smiling good-morning and indicated chairs where they were to sit while she read the Scripture for the day. Then prayers were said, the household dismissed and Bella was sent into the breakfast-room to start her breakfast while her sister remained behind with Mrs. Trantam.

The lady was brisk and businesslike and came at once to the point.

'I understand,' she said as the door closed behind Bella, 'that your father left you two girls without a penny. Is that so?'

'I'm afraid it is.'

'It seems curious that he should have been so improvident. I met him once some years ago when you were all staying in

Brighton, and he struck me then as being a charming man. I know the house—Grey Ladies—where you lived very well. I used to go to balls there in my youth when the Poynters had it. It needs a large income to keep it up, I imagine, but Lady Trantam told me everyone believed your father to be a very rich man.'

Catherine flushed. 'I am afraid he hadn't a very good business head,' she said lamely, and Mrs. Trantam glanced at her sharply as if she guessed there was more behind it than that.

'Well, it's none of my business,' she said drily. 'What does concern me and, indirectly, you, is that I am in need of a companion, and that I am tired of having middle-aged fools clucking round me like hens, unable to read aloud properly, or understand a piece of music, or even to match up embroidery silks without a lot of tedious explanation. Hannah is quite capable of undertaking the more arduous of the duties that have fallen to the lot of my companions in the past, and I have made up my mind to have a younger woman who will be a companion to me in every sense of that misused word. I want somebody with me whom I can treat as I would a daughter, her duties to be no more than those you and your sister must have undertaken at home.'

She paused, watching Catherine, who remained silent, waiting to hear more, and then she continued:

'I should expect her to drive out with me in the carriage, to write notes for me and send out invitations to the small dinner parties and musical evenings that I give from time to time, and to be present, of course, at my At Home days. She might also be required to take a hand at cards in the evenings, and if she liked to have lessons in singing or the piano I would be happy to pay for them, because I am fond of playing the piano myself and enjoy good singing . . . And in return for these services I am prepared to pay a salary of one hundred pounds a year.'

It was three times as much as Catherine could have expected and she was so astonished that she could not speak. Mrs. Trantam took her silence for hesitation, and frowned.

'Are you squeamish about mentioning money, my dear?' she asked with a touch of temper. 'In your position I'm afraid you will have to get used to that, however much it may offend you!'

'On the contrary, your terms are so surprising . . . so generous and kind . . . that I don't know what to say.' Catherine spoke simply and sincerely. 'I feel you may be taking too great a risk . . . You know nothing about us.'

'I have Lady Trantam's recommendation and that is enough. Have you anything else against my offer?'

'I have nothing against it, Mrs. Trantam. How could I? The only thing that troubles me is that I cannot be parted from Bella, so that I shall have to have time in which to find lodgings for her somewhere near Mecklinburgh Square—' She broke off, watching the older woman's face anxiously.

'But I was not thinking of offering the position to *you*, Miss Whittingham!' said Mrs. Trantam calmly. 'I thought you would understand that it was your sister Isabella that I had in mind.'

3

The colour flooded Catherine's face in a shock of surprise, and Mrs. Trantam went on quickly:

'Your sister reminds me of my own daughter, my only child, who died of typhoid fever when she was fifteen. She had Isabella's gentle, timid ways, her fair fragile prettiness and the same gay laugh. From what I have heard and seen of you both I should say that you are far more able to meet misfortune than Isabella, and I am equally sure that she wouldn't find her duties with me too arduous. I hope you agree with me there?'

'Of course I agree with you, Mrs. Trantam. I couldn't wish for anything better for her.' A home as rich and luxurious as the one they had left, and one hundred a year into the bargain for little Bella, who had no more idea of the value of money than the man in the moon. And piano and singing lessons, and musical evenings and At Home days, with Bella trailing about Mrs. Trantam's drawing-room in her pretty dresses and charming everyone there as much as she had done at home—what more could the most loving and anxious of sisters want for her?

'And if I can persuade her that I shall do equally well on my own,' she added aloud, 'I am sure she will be as happy as I am about it.'

'Ah, but *will* you do as well on your own?' demanded Mrs. Trantam with a sharp glance at her. 'Have you anything in mind?'

Catherine admitted that she had nothing in view at the moment.

'Well, then, you may like to consider a proposal I have to make to you after breakfast—but we are keeping Isabella waiting. As I have already breakfasted, I will leave you to join her and tell her in private what I have said so that you can discuss it with her without fear of hurting anybody's feelings.'

Bella's reaction to the news was much as Catherine expected: astonishment that she should have been chosen rather than her far cleverer sister, nervousness lest the duties should be beyond her, apprehension at being parted from Catherine and worry as to what might become of her.

'I shall soon find something to occupy me, darling,' said Catherine consolingly. 'I'm not a bit afraid of that. Life is largely what you make it, and all you need is a lot of cheerfulness and a little courage . . . And, whatever you do, don't *wilt*, love. I'm sure Mrs. Trantam won't take kindly to a wilter!'

Bella laughed, and by the time they joined Mrs. Trantam in the drawing-room a little later she was almost as optimistic as her sister.

Mrs. Trantam was delighted to hear the result of their consultation and kissed Bella and told her that she hoped they would get on well together.

'I see no reason why we shouldn't,' she went on. 'I am sure you are a lovable creature, and I only wish I were as sure of myself. But it is a frustrating business to grow old when your heart remains obstinately young, and such frustration frays the temper and renders one abominably impatient. You must bear with me at such times.' She then summoned the girls to the window, which, like Bella's above it, looked down on the square.

'You must have noticed the house next door when you arrived yesterday,' she said with a wave of her stick at Number Five and addressing Catherine more than her sister, 'if only for its abominable colour. It belongs to Mrs. Ravensbourne, the widow of a wealthy North Country manufacturer. She lives there with an invalid daughter—a pale, dark girl with a discontented face—and her nephew's little girl, Amy. I called on

Mrs. Ravensbourne soon after she came some years ago, but I found her brusque to the point of rudeness, and although I tried to make allowances because her daughter looked so ill, I did not feel encouraged to follow up the acquaintance. There were only a handful of servants in the house then and there are no more now. An elderly female by the name of Pouncer looks after Miss Ravensbourne, and the little girl has governesses, but none of them stay very long.'

'We saw her in the square gardens this morning,' said Bella.

'Yes, I saw her there too. She was with her aunt, Lady Ulsborne—her mother's sister. She comes to see her sometimes when she is staying with her sister-in-law, Lady Selincourt, but she comes early before Mrs. Ravensbourne is up, because there is no love lost between them.'

'We travelled down in the same carriage with Lady Ulsborne yesterday,' said Bella. 'There was a gentleman with her—a dark, unpleasant-looking person.'

'That would be Mr. Ravensbourne, Amy's father. He comes to see his aunt when he can spare the time from the mills. I think they manufacture cloth, but after my call on Mrs. Ravensbourne I did not trouble myself about them until I was introduced to Lady Ulsborne at a concert in Lady Selincourt's drawing-room one evening last summer. But it is cold in this window. Come to the fire where we can talk more comfortably.'

When they were settled by the fire she went on: 'After Lady Ulsborne discovered that I was Mrs. Ravensbourne's neighbour she became very friendly and told me that she thought her little niece was being very much neglected. She said that Amy's father cared nothing about her, and that the governesses Mrs. Ravensbourne engaged for the child never stayed more than a few weeks. At that time she was being cared for entirely by a rough maid—Maggie by name—with far too much to do to be able to spare much time for her, and her "education" consisted solely in learning how to mend Mrs. Ravensbourne's household linen. I asked Lady Ulsborne why she did not speak to her brother-in-law about it, and she said she had tried to bring it to his notice, but without any result, but that recently she had heard of a Frenchwoman who had been governess to the children of some friends of hers in London and was looking for another situation. She thought she would ask Mr. Ravensbourne if she might engage her for little Amy, and as I saw the child afterwards in the company of a woman who, by her appearance and manner, suggested a foreigner I concluded she had been successful, and thought no more about it until this letter came a little while ago.'

She went to her desk and produced a letter from a pigeon-hole under the flap. 'I kept it because I felt I might be able to help her, although at the time I did not know how. She told me in it that Mademoiselle was leaving after a stay of six months, and she said—let me see if I can find it—yes, here it is! *If you should come across a lady, and I mean a lady, because no one else would stay, who would be prepared to love and look after my poor sister's little girl in the face of hardship and neglect, will you please write to me at once, dear Mrs. Trantam? Because I am now quite sure that if I don't replace Mademoiselle at Number Five nobody else will.*'

Mrs. Trantam folded the letter and put it away.

'I believe in being honest about things, and I must say that Lady Ulsborne did not strike me as being a person to feel deeply over anything, and I thought her concern over her niece might be quickly roused and just as quickly forgotten. But since hearing from her I have made it my business to watch my little neighbour from time to time, and she does look a poor, thin little creature and very badly dressed. I seldom see her out with the maid, but I have caught sight of her little face pressed to one of the attic windows sometimes, as if she were a prisoner there, so that when I heard about you two girls it occurred to me that here were three people I could help—Lady Ulsborne, her little niece and a young lady who found herself to be suddenly in need of employment.' Her eyes rested significantly on Catherine. 'What might be beyond the powers of a French mademoiselle might not be beyond those of the daughter of General Whittingham!'

Catherine remained silent, too astonished at the unexpected turn the conversation had taken to be able to say anything, and Mrs. Trantam went on: 'I wrote to Lady Ulsborne suggesting that I should offer you the situation when you arrived, giving her the date when you were coming to Brighton, and in the letter I received from her by return of post she said she would come to Brighton and interview you herself at eleven o'clock this morning.'

She looked at Catherine with an air of pleased satisfaction and failed to observe the dismay on Bella's face as she heard of this high-handed disposal of her elder sister's affairs. When they had discussed their future at Grey Ladies they had decided that the post of governess was not to be considered by either of them: they would be prepared to give private lessons in music, singing and languages, and Catherine had even thought of turning her hand to journalism. Her Aunt Ellen in Putney knew a lady journalist who made as much as ten shillings a week by writing little articles for the newspapers, and the examples she had sent her to read had been so extremely bad that she was certain she could do better.

But in throwing herself and Bella upon the goodwill of Mrs. Henry Trantam she no more expected that her kindness would have taken this unkind turn than she could have dreamed, in listening to the conversation in the railway carriage the day before, that the governess the lady in the sables was coming to Brighton to see could possibly be herself.

As she sat silent, not knowing how to express her feelings without sounding ungrateful and ungracious, there came the sound of a carriage stopping outside and a few minutes later Lady Ulsborne was shown upstairs and into the room.

*   *   *

It seemed to Catherine afterwards that from that moment a force outside her control took charge of her future and swept her along with it: there was no time to protest, and she did not think that anybody would have listened if she had.

Lady Ulsborne, after a glance of startled recognition, bowed an acknowledgement of Mrs. Trantam's introduction and held out her hand to the elder Miss Whittingham.

'You travelled down with us!' she exclaimed. 'When I saw you sitting there I hoped that the lady Mrs. Trantam recommended would be somebody like you!' The words appeared to be sincere, and the manner in which they were spoken was so friendly that Catherine's resentment faded. She said smiling:

'But, Lady Ulsborne, I have never been a governess in my life! I would be an utter amateur at the business . . . and, in fact, I really don't know how I should start.'

'Oh, nonsense!' Lady Ulsborne brushed her protest aside. 'Anybody can be a governess—anybody, that is, who has had governesses of their own, as I'm sure you have had in the past! All you have to do is to sit at the schoolroom table and teach Amy how to read and write, and to take her for walks along the front, and . . . to persuade one of the maids to mend her clothes. Her heels were out of her stockings this morning! I was ashamed to let the groom see them!'

Mrs. Trantam here interrupted impatiently. 'I have told Miss Whittingham about your poor little niece, Lady Ulsborne,' she said. 'And I know she will be glad to help you if she can. Anybody of her capabilities could be governess to a child of eight years old.'

'You see, Miss Whittingham,' went on Lady Ulsborne, 'from what Mademoiselle told me when she was there I'm pretty sure that from the time I leave Brighton today until I come again nobody in that dreadful house will wash the child's face or run a comb through her hair. Mrs. Ravensbourne has never had a scrap of affection for Amy, and yet when my husband and I offered to adopt her and bring her up with our own children my brother-in-law refused to consider it. He said that he trusted his aunt completely and that she hid a warm heart under an unyielding exterior, but all I can say is that she hides it very well, because nobody would ever suspect that she possessed a heart at all!'

She paused with a small indignant laugh, and Catherine was silent, a prey to a mixture of feelings in which the easy assumption of both Mrs. Trantam and Lady Ulsborne that she must be willing to fall in with any situation, however uninviting, was almost forgotten in the problem that faced her. After all, she thought sadly, who was Miss Whittingham now that she could choose what she wanted to do? Her services were as much in the open market as those of the smallest servant-girl.

Lady Ulsborne went on in the same half-exaggerated, half-indignant fashion as before: 'I must warn you that your salary will be small—my dear brother-in-law doesn't part lightly with his "brass". And the food will be vile, and the servants will do as little as they can for you. I don't know when I've met a more disobliging creature than that Pouncer! You will be frozen in the winter and stifled in the summer, and slighted by everybody . . . I know you won't stay. Nobody *could* stay under such conditions! But I keep hoping that by some miracle my brother-in-law will change his mind and let me have Amy by and by. She is a dainty little thing and I'd dress her so prettily, and the poor mite is so fond of me. The tears were brimming over in her eyes when she parted from me this morning, but Maggie was waiting to let her in and I had to go, because Mrs. Ravensbourne is so rude when we meet that it upsets me and sets my nerves on edge for weeks.'

Catherine's common sense told her that it would be stupid to embark on the first thing that offered, and that it might be better to risk Mrs. Trantam's displeasure and Lady Ulsborne's disappointment than rush into a situation that promised to be so difficult and unpleasant. She had met many Lady Ulsbornes among her own friends in the past: young fashionable married women who declared that they adored their children, and yet were thankful to hand them back to their nurses and governesses after half an hour of their society in the drawing-room after tea. She did not think that Lady Ulsborne's concern for her little niece would last until her train had drawn out of Brighton station, but in that moment of indecision she couldn't help remembering the child's face that morning, when she had drawn her aunt's arm round her neck, and the shrinking air of reluctance with which she had climbed the steps of the house next door, and pity and curiosity fought with common sense and won. She found herself saying as calmly as if she had considered it from every angle before making up her mind, 'When would you like me to begin my duties, Lady Ulsborne?'

Mrs. Trantam smiled approval, and Lady Ulsborne said quickly, before she could have time to repent, 'Can you start this afternoon, at four o'clock?'

Catherine agreed to be on the doorstep as the clock struck four, and Lady Ulsborne sat down at once at Mrs. Trantam's desk to write a note to Mrs. Ravensbourne to acquaint her of the new governess's arrival.

'I daresay Amy will be looking for you,' she added as she sealed the note, and Mrs. Trantam rang the bell for one of her servants to take it next door. '*If* they remember to tell her that you are coming! It would not surprise me if they didn't, because the boot-boy, Albert, gets more consideration in that house than she does. But one can only do one's best under the circumstances.' And then, feeling no doubt that she had done all that could be expected of her, she said goodbye and hurried away. As they watched her carriage drive briskly to the corner and disappear, Mrs. Trantam said she was delighted that it had all been settled so quickly.

'There's nothing like knowing where you stand,' she added. 'And if an unpleasant thing like earning our own living has to be faced, then the sooner you start the better.'

She spoke with such authority that nobody would have thought she was the only child of a very rich man, and one, moreover, who had never had to think of earning her own living under any circumstances. When the two girls were sent out for a walk along the sea-front before lunch, however,

Catherine found herself becoming more reconciled to the prospect in front of her. If it had nothing else to recommend it, at least it would free Mrs. Trantam from the embarrassment of her presence in her house.

Bella was not nearly so pleased.

'I know Mrs. Trantam meant it kindly,' she said as they made their way towards the West Pier, 'but I do wish she had allowed you to make your own arrangements, Kate. I don't like to think of you being hurried into this queer situation next door. Mrs. Ravensbourne sounds a most unpleasant person—quite as unpleasant as her nephew.'

'But as he does not live there I am not likely to meet him, and there is no need for you to worry your head about his aunt. Thanks to Mr. Jason I am free to "give in my notice" at any time I please.'

'I can't understand why Mr. Ravensbourne won't let Lady Ulsborne adopt little Amy. It would be much better for the child than living miserably here in Brighton with that horrid old aunt.'

'I expect there is some reason for it. There generally is a reason for odd behaviour.'

'Do you think he was so broken-hearted when his wife died that he wouldn't hear of his little girl being adopted?' said Bella hopefully.

'We don't know that Mr. Ravensbourne's wife is dead. She may have divorced her husband.'

'Kate!' Bella was horrified. 'How can you think of such a thing? Lady Ulsborne is a lady ... I'm sure her sister would never be involved in anything so sordid as a divorce!'

'Poor, romantic Bella! Not all marriages are "happy ever after", darling! And I'm afraid that Lady Ulsborne knows a great deal more than she is prepared to say about the household next door. I thought she was a little mysterious about it, because in all her tirade against her brother-in-law and his aunt, and in spite of her so-called devotion to little Amy, one thing emerged very plainly—she never said anything at all about her sister. I waited for her to say, "My sister died when Amy was a year old", or something of the sort, but she didn't, and it struck me as being extremely odd.'

'I don't see anything odd about it.' Bella frowned uneasily. 'One doesn't tell strangers all about one's family in the first few moments of meeting them.'

'I know. But usually a prospective employer will tell a governess—even such an amateur one as I am—all she needs to know about the parents of her charge, otherwise how is the poor woman to avoid embarrassing situations?'

'Kate! I hate to hear you talk about "employers" like that. It sounds so . . . poor . . . and commonplace.'

'But I *am* poor and commonplace now, my love, and, as Mrs. Trantam pointed out just now, we have to face these things! A mountain doesn't become smaller just by turning one's back on it. It's still there and just as large . . . Don't look reproachful and unhappy, darling. We'll pretend a little, if it pleases you better. We'll say that I'm going on a visit to Mrs. Ravensbourne next door, that the little girl there is excellently looked after, that all marriages are made in heaven and divorce does not exist.'

'Now you are laughing at me. And you can say what you like, but I shall never understand how any lady—real lady, that is—*could* consent to a divorce.'

'Yet some of them do, Bella, my pet. I wish I were one of these strong-minded females ready to take up the cudgels for my sex, but I'm not. Do you know, Bella, a man may divorce his wife for unfaithfulness, but a wife cannot divorce her husband for the same reason unless she can prove cruelty as well? And what woman with any decent feeling is going into a law court to say that her husband gave her a pair of black eyes, like a Billingsgate porter on a Saturday night?'

'I expect it's because men sit in Parliament and make all the laws that they're unfair to women,' said Bella comfortably. 'But I'm very glad they do—sit in Parliament, I mean. I'm sure *I* wouldn't want to be bothered with such things! I shall marry a rich man, who will give me everything I want, including a maid to do my hair!'

'As long as he gives you love as well I won't grudge him to you, darling.'

'Who's being romantic now?' Bella caught her sister's hand and laughed. 'And here we are at the entrance to the pier . . . Is there time to have a walk to the end of it before lunch?'

There was time, and Catherine smilingly paid at the turnstile and they hurried through, their faces bright with the moment's excitement. A man who was just coming off the pier stood aside to let them pass, and sent a second glance after them that had surprise and admiration in it.

They did not see him, however. In the exhilaration of walking on the echoing planks with the sea beneath them and the wind almost taking their hats from their heads, their spirits rose, and they were able to forget that Catherine was to say goodbye to her sister that afternoon for the first time in their lives.

*   *   *

William Ravensbourne made his way towards his aunt's house with a thoughtful look on his face.

Who would have thought that those two girls were the same as the sorrowful creatures who had sat quietly in the same railway carriage with himself and Helen yesterday? Then he had considered the taller, dark one to be a discontented young woman, and he had resented the small smile that touched her lips as she listened to his conversation with Lady Ulsborne, suspecting patronage. But today there was no aloofness in that pale face: it was animated and alive, smiling and tender. He wondered who they were, and what close relative they had lost recently enough to plunge them into such deep mourning.

He crossed the road, making for Mecklinburgh Square, and passed a carriage that was standing outside a shop, and at the same moment a familiar figure came out of the shop. She was about to get into the carriage when she turned her head and saw him.

'Will!' she cried. 'Come here, Will! I want to speak to you.'

He waited until the groom had shut her into the carriage and returned to his seat beside the coachman, and then, rather unwillingly, he came to the window, where she greeted him with a dazzling smile.

'I congratulate you, Will!' she cried. 'Or perhaps I should say you must congratulate me!'

He smiled in spite of himself. There were times when Helen could be very fascinating. 'Let us congratulate each other, then,' he said.

'I have interviewed Miss Whittingham,' she said, 'and she is charming and capable. You remember those two girls in the carriage with us yesterday? One dark and slender, and the other a little fair, plump creature, with her face all tear-stains under her veil?'

'I did not notice the tear-stains,' he said rather stiffly, his smile fading. 'I saw them both just now off for a walk on the pier, and they looked a great deal happier.'

'And no wonder, because the little one has just been engaged as Mrs. Henry Trantam's companion, and the elder one—the dark one—is going to be Amy's governess!'

'Amy's governess!' His dismay was so apparent that she laughed.

'Don't look so scared, Will! You'll never see her... and she will stand no nonsense from your aunt! I told you coming down in the train that she was a General's daughter! Little did we think she was sitting a few feet away from us all the time!'

He felt there was nobody that Helen could have picked on that he wanted less to teach his daughter in his aunt's house.

'Well?' said Helen impatiently. 'Aren't you going to thank me?'

'I am a Yorkshireman,' he replied. 'With a Yorkshireman's caution . . . I never give thanks until I know if they are due. But it was kindly meant, Helen, and for that I will thank you with all my heart.'

She looked at him strangely, her own worldly little heart touched for a second by a feeling of compassion and guilt. 'Poor Will!' she said gently. 'My family has been a thorn in your side ever since that first unlucky house party when Terry brought you down from Oxford to stay with us. If I can do anything to repay our debt to you I'll do it . . . I want Richard to take a house here for the summer, and I would like to ask Amy to come and see her cousins then, but I know it is impossible.'

'I don't understand you. Why should it be impossible?'

'I don't know why . . . but it will be. You will see . . . At least I have your permission to invite her?'

'Of course.'

'Thank you, I'll remember that.' And then she signalled to the coachman to drive on.

He arrived at Number Five soon after twelve, and was admitted by a breathless Maggie, who told him that her mistress was upstairs in Miss Edith's room.

'I'll go up to her, then.' He climbed the dark stairs and found his aunt alone in the large drawing-room that was reserved for his Cousin Edith's use. Like the other rooms in that house, it never had a window open, and as usual the heat from the enormous fire and the scent of the flowers that filled the vases met him like the cloying atmosphere of a conservatory.

'Good morning, William.' Mrs. Ravensbourne receiving his kiss ungraciously. 'Poor Edith is not well, so I am keeping her in bed until after luncheon. I have had a note from that wretched sister-in-law of yours saying she has found a new governess for Amy. Helen Ulsborne is never happy unless she is meddling in other people's business.'

'She spoke to me about it and asked my consent, and knowing how hard you have found it to get suitable governesses for the child I had little hesitation in giving it.'

'But I don't consider a General's daughter to be a suitable governess for Amy!' said his aunt austerely. 'If she thinks she is going to play the grand lady here I shall disabuse her of that right away.'

'I understood from Helen that the young lady has been left in a position where she is forced to earn her living, so that she will not be likely to put on airs under such circumstances. And Amy must have a governess—unless you consider her to be old enough to begin school?'

'Oh no, certainly not!' Mrs. Ravensbourne quickly changed the subject. 'We will give this Miss Whittingham a trial, and I daresay she will do for a time. But you didn't come to see me about anything so trivial as Amy's education, I am sure?'

'No. That was only a secondary consideration. I go back to Yorkshire tomorrow and I would like to know if you have given further thought to the matter we talked of the last time I was here?'

'I thought that was what had brought you.' Her eyes were shrewd. 'Well, you could have saved yourself the journey. There are enough old servants left at the Mills to keep me informed of what goes on there, and my answer is still that I will never be a party to such folly.'

Her nephew frowned impatiently. 'How can you call it folly when you have had only a garbled account from people who know nothing about the true facts of the case? Let me at least show you the outline of my plan.' He took a bundle of papers from his pocket, but she waved them aside.

'I don't want to see it. You can wrap it up in whatever words you like, William, but the outcome is the same. You have got this wild idea that the Ravensbourne Mills—founded by your great-great-grandfather in his own cottage over a hundred years ago—should be handed over to the work-people under some co-operative scheme that could make them masters where they should be servants.'

William Ravensbourne gave a slightly scornful smile. 'My dear aunt, your spies should do better than this! We have a great deal of capital tied up in the mills, you and I and my two brothers. We don't want more than five per cent interest on that money—which would yield us all extremely good incomes. But as the business expands—and Ravensbourne's *is* expanding all the time—so the management and owners are faced with labour troubles—better wages and shorter hours elsewhere, and so on. These problems will get larger and more complex as time goes on, and to my mind there is only one solution. At the end of each year, when money has been deducted for improvements and expansion of plant and so on, and five per cent paid out on the capital invested, instead of the owners dividing the profits, as we have done in the past, I want those profits issued as bonus shares to our work-people. If we give them cash they will only spend it: shares will encourage thrift and give them pride in the mills—the pride of ownership —or partnership, if you prefer it. Don't you understand, Aunt Anna? Taylors have done it, and they're not the only ones. Several more have followed their lead.'

'Including one or two that have gone bankrupt! Happen you've forgotten them—conveniently!'

'I've forgotten nothing, and I know the risk involved. Last year we didn't pay a dividend, and this year looks to be as bad, although the old Queen's Jubilee is doing good abroad, and orders are already coming in again. But we've had bad years before this and weathered them, and I believe if one takes one's work-people into one's confidence at such times they'll understand. They've far more brains than you give them credit for, Aunt Anna.'

'Well, to me it's crass folly and the certain ruin of a magnificent business—one that your own flesh and blood created out of nothing. You will throw it away. I'm not surprised at your brothers, they haven't your intelligence and never had your education. I was always against you going to Oxford, mind. I said no good would come of it at the time. But I never thought you'd be as stupid as this. Why, your father and my husband would turn in their graves.'

'So you won't consider spreading the profits in such a way?'

'Never. I will never consent to it, and as I still hold a large share of the firm's capital I don't think you'll be able to do anything without my consent, William.'

He shrugged his shoulders and walked to the window and stared down at the gardens for a moment before he said abruptly, 'Unless I buy you out.'

'What!' She was incredulous. 'Don't you remember the terms of your father's will—that if at any time you wished to purchase my interest in the firm you would pay me one half of the capital that was left in it at his death? It may not have been as large then as it is now, but I seem to recall that it amounted to every penny of eighty thousand pounds, and that is the sum you would have to pay me now, my lad. I don't think even your pocket is as deep as that!'

'With the bank's help I might be able to find it. We shall see.'

'You think the bank would advance you eighty thousand pounds, knowing what you intend to do with your profits in the future?'

'The bank knows me.'

'But such a debt would ruin you.' She added more kindly, 'Will, my dear, I don't want to rob you of your brass any more than I want to see a fine old firm brought down.' He remained obstinately silent, and she added shortly, 'Do you want to see Amy before you go?'

'No. I'll see her the next time I'm here.' He picked up his hat and cane and went to the door, and there he turned to smile at his aunt, his eyes bright with challenge. 'I'm not giving up, though. I intend to go on with this.'

'Eh, I guessed that.' Her voice was half grudging, half angry. 'You're a fighter, Will . . . I know that. But I'm a fighter too. Happen you'll remember that as well!'

And so they parted, antagonists, but in a queer way enjoying the coming battle in advance, as they had often done in the past.

As he walked down the square a small, white face at an attic window watched him go, its nose flattened against the pane and its eyes following him until he was out of sight.

4

No curtain moved behind the windows of Number Five when Catherine mounted the steps of that inhospitable house at four o'clock that afternoon, and even the fickle sun had disappeared. It was drizzling with rain again and the sea was grey under a lowering sky, the mournful cries of the gulls as they wheeled and dived against it giving warning of more bad weather to come.

She knocked twice and stood there for some minutes before the door was opened by a tall woman in black.

'Good afternoon,' said Catherine. 'I am Miss Whittingham.'

'The governess,' said the woman sourly, staring at her as if she had no right to be there. 'Come in.'

Catherine followed her into the silent hall, half expecting to see little Amy in the shadows, waiting for her, but hall and stairs were empty, and the maid shut and bolted the front door before showing her into a small, dark room on the right. No fire burned there, and the chill of the room after the warmth of Mrs. Trantam's house struck into the very bones of the amateur governess. Three books were arranged with mathematical precision on a table in the window, the chairs and settee, upholstered in horsehair, looked so hard and slippery that she felt they would repel any attempt at sitting on them, there was a mirror in a black frame over the chimney-piece, and beneath it a black marble clock was flanked by two bronze urns that might have been receptacles for funeral ashes. Two brackets holding gas-jets protected by plain glass globes were on either side of the chimney, and the floor was covered with brown drugget, over a carpet of a quality evidently too superior to see the light of day.

The dreadful little room and the lack of taste in its furnishings were as alien to Catherine as the house and its inmates promised to be, and with a sinking heart she looked about her and thought she must have been mad to come there. Brighton lodgings and piano lessons would be preferable to teaching a child of whom she knew nothing in such surroundings, and she had made up her mind to leave at the first opportunity even before Mrs. Ravensbourne descended the stairs with creaking majesty to join her.

Amy's great-aunt was a massive woman, with iron-grey hair parted in the middle and dressed in a bun on top of her head. Her face was large, her complexion slightly mottled, her eyes light grey, her lips thin. She was dressed in a purple cloth dress of excellent quality, but over-trimmed and badly cut, and it did not suit her complexion. Her hands were plump, their square-tipped fingers covered in rings, and round her neck was a three-stranded jet necklace. Several gold bracelets of heavy design clasped her wrists like fetters.

She acknowledged Catherine's greeting with a sharp nod, and she did not offer to shake hands, nor did she ask her to be seated. She was a singularly ungracious woman.

'So you are Miss Whittingham!' Her cold little eyes examined Catherine's dress and hat. 'Lady Ulsborne said you were a General's daughter.'

Catherine flushed under the sneer that accompanied the words and replied quietly: 'My father was General Whittingham. He served with distinction in several campaigns—'

'I daresay he did, but I've no time to listen to them.' Mrs. Ravensbourne cut her short abruptly. 'It's no good colouring up. I speak my mind and if it don't suit you I can't help it. You may be a General's daughter—I am a manufacturer's daughter, and none the worse for that—but you need not think that you can behave as a guest in my house.'

Catherine would have liked to reply that under no circumstances could she imagine herself as being Mrs. Ravensbourne's guest, but she held her tongue, and her silence angered the lady still more, as she took it for further evidence of pride. She went on in a harsher tone:

'You are here to look after my great-niece, and you are to take full responsibility for her. Please understand that. I want to have nothing to do with her, or with you. I don't want to see or hear her: her health is your concern, her happiness concerns nobody. The moment you come whining to me about her lack of friends, or that she should have other children in to tea, or some such nonsense, you will go. My nephew, Mr. William Ravensbourne, provides her board and lodging and yours, and he only requires that I should accommodate you both in my house.'

'I understand.' Catherine's dark eyes met the hostile ones calmly. 'Your house appears to be a large one, and I see no reason why you should see or hear Amy. I will certainly do my best to keep her out of your way.'

'Then we shall not fall out.' Slightly more graciously Mrs. Ravensbourne dismissed her to the elderly maid, who had been waiting in the hall and listening to the conversation with malicious delight through the half-open door. 'Take Miss Whittingham upstairs, Pouncer, and then come back and get Miss Edith's tea.'

'Yes, ma'am.' The maid led the way upstairs and as they reached the wide corridor at the top of the first flight Catherine caught a fleeting glimpse of a large drawing-room filled with vases of spring flowers, and a young woman with a pale, unhappy face, wrapped in a rug and seated on a sofa in front of a cheerfully blazing fire. Then Pouncer hurried her on to a red baize door that shut off the back staircase and servants' quarters, where she stopped, and opening the baize door called down the stairs: 'Maggie! Come up here at once!'

While they waited Catherine said pleasantly, 'If you are busy, Pouncer, I'll wait here for Maggie.'

The woman stared at her with a hostility equal to that of her mistress. '*Miss* Pouncer to you!' she said insolently.

Catherine had dealt with impertinent servants once or twice in her life, but this was not the time or place to do it, on her first afternoon in Mrs. Ravensbourne's house. So she ignored it and waited until a big untidy country girl, with a pretty face marred by several black smudges, came running up the stairs. Catherine was delivered into her charge and they went on together, up the back stairs, past more closed baize doors, until they came to a little winding, scrubbed wooden staircase, devoid of carpet, and leading directly up to the attics that ran across the top of the house.

In spite of Lady Ulsborne's account of her niece's treatment, Catherine had imagined nothing like this, and she followed Maggie up this last flight in silent amazement until they reached the top, where for the first time in their climb the stillness of the house was broken by the sound of a child singing.

Maggie paused with a friendly smile.

'Here we are.' She gave a nod towards a doorway through which Catherine saw what she took to be an empty garret until her eyes grew accustomed to the light that came in through a skylight and one far, uncurtained dormer window, and then she found it was in reality a series of small attic rooms, each leading out of the other across the top of the house.

'So,' she commented in a low voice, 'Mrs. Ravensbourne puts her little great-niece into the attics?'

'It's a shame,' Maggie agreed, shaking her head. 'There's a whole floor empty just below this . . . But we do what we can for her, me and Albert, though it's little we can do really, poor little thing.'

'I'm sure you do everything you are able to do,' said Catherine warmly, and went on into the room.

The attics ran from front to back of the house, and at the far end, skirts held out as she danced gravely to her singing, was the child she had seen in the gardens that morning. She was dressed in an ugly grey dress, much too old for her years, and, like the brown coat she had worn over it, it was also a great deal too small for her. Her black woollen stockings were green with age and had large holes in the heels, and her shoes were almost through at the toes. Her arms and legs were like matchsticks, and her pale little face was smudged round the eyes as if she had been crying, although now she was wholly absorbed by what she was doing. 'One, two, three, skip!' and in between these orders to her feet she sang a queer, haunting little tune.

Catherine glanced about her, her amazement deepening every moment. Two wooden chairs stood on either side of a plain deal table covered with American cloth, on which were a couple of books of old-fashioned moral tales, left open as if the reader had grown weary of them. On the floor a broken doll was thrown against an old fender that shielded a fireplace in which a fire had burnt itself out, and a piece of candle with a long winding sheet of wax was stuck in a cracked china candlestick on the chimney-piece. An empty bookcase completed the room's furniture and as she remembered the flower-filled room downstairs Catherine thought she had never seen an apartment so bare and comfortless and inhuman.

Then Maggie called to the little girl and she stopped dancing and whirled round, her eyes going from the housemaid to Catherine.

'Oh!' she said. 'My new governess!' She dropped her skirt

and came up with a few little dancing steps, but without a flicker of a smile, and her eyes were older than any child's should be.

'Now then, Miss Amy,' said Maggie kindly. 'Say good afternoon nicely to Miss Whittingham.'

'And how do you say good afternoon nicely, Maggie?' said Amy in a shrill little voice, and put her head on one side and gave Catherine a slanting, impudent look. 'You are younger than Mamzelle, and you are nicer to look at . . . but I wonder how long you'll stay?'

'Now, Miss Amy,' said Maggie again, 'that's not the way to speak to a lady.'

'She's not a lady,' said the child contemptuously. 'She's a governess . . . And you needn't think I shall care about her any more than I cared about the others. She won't stay any longer than they stayed, and that's why I don't intend to interest myself in her. She can go away again this very night if she wants to: *I* shan't stop her. I'd much rather have you and Albert!' And she danced away down the succession of little rooms, her ugly dress taking a steely light from the March afternoon.

'I'm sorry she spoke to you like that,' said Maggie in a low voice. 'And she knows she's not allowed to dance. She's just being naughty. Don't be angry with her.'

'I wouldn't dream of being angry with her,' said Catherine gently. 'I expect she's frightened.'

'Frightened?' The maid looked at her quickly.

'Of being left alone,' explained Catherine, smiling. 'It's natural for a child to be boisterous and rude when it's afraid. When I was small I used to shout every time I went into a dark room, just to bolster up my courage.'

Maggie nodded, but it seemed there was something else on her mind, of which she did not speak.

Catherine prompted her, 'And why is she not allowed to dance?'

'Missus's strict orders,' said Maggie with an air of relief at being able to speak of something she knew about. 'She's not to be taught dancing, nor to be allowed to dance at any time. Missus came up here one day and caught her at it and whipped her till the blood came. That's what really decided Mamzelle to leave . . . But you might as well tell the sun not to shine as tell Miss Amy not to dance. She's always dancing, up here where nobody can see her, and her feet are so light you can scarcely hear them at all, can you? Missus would never have

45

found her that day if old Pouncer hadn't told her. At least, I suppose it was Pouncer, because I don't know who else it could have been.' She broke off. 'I'm sorry, miss. I ought not to be standing here, talking ... I'll fetch your tea.'

'Do we have it up here? Is this the schoolroom?'

'I'm afraid it is, miss.' The girl was apologetic. 'We don't like coming all this way with the meals, I can tell you. There's only me and Albert to do it, and it's a long climb from the kitchens in the basement. The old nurseries and schoolroom were on the floor below, and what use are they, shut up and empty, with the child up here day after day with not a soul to speak to? Her own mother's sister only comes twice or so in the year!'

'But surely her father comes oftener?'

'If he does he only sees her downstairs when he comes to see the Missus on business, and then sometimes he'll only remember to ask for Miss Amy just before he goes. "I hope you are being good," he says, giving her two fingers to shake. "And I hope you are doing your lessons." And off he goes without a kiss or another look. You'd think he hated her. I'm leaving when my two years are up. They can't say I haven't a character then, and I want a place where I'm paid a living wage, and not worked to death, and have to stand by and see a little thing like that so cruelly done by. It's not what I'm used to, miss. My father is a fisherman, and often we've not had much beyond a crust of bread to put into our mouths, but we've had love all our lives, and that's what children need.'

She went off down the stairs and Catherine sat down in the chair that had arms to it, and out of the corner of her eye she noticed that the dancing feet had faltered a little before going on with their steps more defiantly still. She said quietly: 'What a nice large space you've got to yourself up here. I expect you can see the sea from that window, can't you?'

The dancing feet paused for a slightly longer moment. 'Why do you trouble yourself to talk to me?' said the child rudely. 'I'm sure I don't want to talk to you!'

'I don't suppose you do. Little girls seldom want to talk to grown-ups. But I would like you to tell me, please, how long your other governesses stayed with you?'

Amy screwed up her face in an effort at remembering. 'Some were here a month, some two, some only a week, and there was Miss-Cooper-who-only-stayed-a-day. She said she was used to having footmen to wait on her, and a schoolroom that was like a drawing-room, but Albert said he didn't believe her.' The feet continued their dancing, but now they were coming towards her.

'And how long did Mamzelle stay?' asked Catherine, and the dancing suddenly stopped.

'I don't know,' said Amy shrilly. 'I don't want to talk about her . . .' The old Frenchwoman who had been devoted to her, who had left because she was whipped 'till the blood came', leaving utter loneliness and grief behind.

'I think she was here six months,' said Amy at last in a shaken little voice.

'I wonder what I can do,' said Catherine briskly, 'to show you that I'm as good a governess as she was?'

Under the untidy hair the child's face lost its look of desolation and became more alert. She came up to the table and leant on her elbows on its top, frowning up at Catherine.

'I don't believe you are a governess,' she said. 'You aren't dressed like one!'

Catherine laughed. 'How did you guess?' she asked.

'Guess what?' But the frown began to fade a little.

'Why, that I'm not a governess at all? You'll have to show me what to do, so that nobody finds out!'

She saw the brown eyes lose their wickedness and become eager and human, and the little face lit up with a warm smile. Then, as the memory of those other governesses — and particularly Mademoiselle — came back to her mind, the smile vanished.

'Why should I show you?' she said, and started to dance again with the swaying grace that Catherine had first noticed in her. One, two, three, skip . . . one, two, three, skip . . . down the length of the attic floor. Presently she came back and went on as if she had never left her, 'Why should I trouble myself about you when you won't stay?'

Was there a quiver in the voice, a hidden longing for a companionship that would not take itself off after a few months, or even weeks? Catherine forgot her decision in the bleak little room downstairs that she would leave this inhospitable house as soon as she decently could. She was reminded of the birds in winter, coming for crumbs to the windows at Grey Ladies and taking them from her hands because starvation had overcome their fear of the humans within, and it seemed to her that this child would approach for crumbs, too, if her heart were not already starved to death.

'If Mademoiselle stayed for six months,' she said firmly, 'it seems to me that I shall have to stay for seven . . . I might even stay longer than seven . . . who knows?'

The child shook her head and said in a flat little voice: 'No, you won't. You'll go just as all the others did!'

'But why did they go?' asked Catherine, and the brown eyes met hers mournfully.

'I expect because they didn't want to stay.' And Amy went back to her dancing. She had turned her back on the crumbs, but they were still there within her reach.

A pot of weak tea, some thin-looking milk, and a few slices of bread with butter scraped thinly across them, were brought up to them by the house-boy, Albert, a lad of fourteen with a face lavishly sprinkled with freckles and a shock of fair hair.

'Missus said I was to light your fire,' he told Catherine, 'seeing as it's your first evening.'

She thanked him. 'It would certainly be more cheerful,' she agreed.

'I'll bring you some extra coals while I'm at it,' added the boy with a knowing wink. 'I'll store 'em in the cupboard, like I did for Mamzelle, then you'll have something to fall back on if it turns colder and the scuttle's empty. Missus is close with coals—except in Miss Edith's rooms.' He went on brightly: 'I've taken your box to your room, miss. It's on the floor below, on the other side of the baize door, afore you get to the old nurseries. Anything you want, you just tell me or Maggie. I can't say as you'll get it, mind, but that depends on what you ask for, don't it?'

Catherine agreed that it did, and gave him a shilling. 'I won't forget your kindness, Albert . . . nor Maggie's,' she said, and was conscious that she was being watched jealously, and guessed it was because Albert and Maggie were the only creatures who had broken the long hours of the child's day or given her any sense of security.

When he had gone she set out the cups and saucers on the American cloth and made a mental note to write to Anthony requesting that some of her belongings should be sent to her from Trantam Court.

'Won't you come and have your tea?' she said, as Amy stood by the window at the far end of the room staring out at the sea. A subdued voice answered her:

'No, thank you. I'm not hungry.'

'What shall I do with your bread and butter then? Shall I

keep it in the cupboard with the coals, in case you don't get any tomorrow?' The child turned her head quickly, and then, seeing her smile, went back to her solitary contemplation of the sea.

'I don't mind what you do with it,' she said indifferently. 'It's all the same to me. But if you put it in the cupboard the mice will have it. They ate the birthday cake that Mamzelle bought for me.' The indifference gave place to anger and grief. 'I'd never had a birthday cake before.'

Catherine poured out a cup of tea for herself and ate a piece of bread-and-butter and did not wonder that the child had refused it, because the bread was stale and the butter rancid. After a moment or two, however, Amy came up to the table reluctantly and sat down on the remaining chair, and taking a piece of bread she began to eat it hungrily. Catherine poured a second cup for her without comment, and said, 'After tea you must show me your lesson books.'

Amy stared. 'I haven't got any,' she said. 'Mamzelle took them with her.'

'Oh!' The amateur governess felt herself to be rather at a loss. 'But I expect you have some exercise books to show me . . . books in which you have written your lessons and done your sums, and so on?'

'I've only got a slate and that's broken. I used to write dictation and French translation in some lesson books, but one day when we were out for a walk somebody burnt them all. So Mamzelle said a slate would be better.'

'But . . . who burnt your books?'

'I don't know.' The child met her incredulity with the same indifference she had exhibited over the fate of her tea. 'I expect it was Great-Aunt Anna. She burnt the book of fairy-tales that Aunt Helen sent me: she said it was rubbish and that I could have two of the books she had when she was my age, but I don't like them very much. They aren't very interesting.'

'And have you no toys? Is that doll the only one you have?'

'Yes, but I don't much care for dolls. Aunt Helen gave me a lovely one, with a wax face and real, French-embroidered clothes, but Great-Aunt Anna gave it away to a church bazaar. She said it was a sin for a child to have an expensive toy like that to destroy, but I wouldn't have destroyed it, truly. It was such a beautiful doll.' She sent a sideways glance at Catherine. 'So I make believe with my sea-shells. I've got a tin box full of them, and I keep them downstairs in my cupboard where

nobody will look for them. There are big ones and little ones
... I pretend they're families ... mothers and fathers and
children, you know. There aren't any aunts or cousins or
governesses, though ... just families. I'll show them to you
someday ... if you stay.' She gave a little sigh, finished her tea
and went back to her dancing.

5

Catherine did not forget her first night at Number Five. Her
room and Amy's were next door to each other at the end of a
long corridor on the third floor, tiny apartments that might
have been used as sewing-rooms in the old days. They were
scantily furnished, and the few articles in them looked as if
they had been taken from the servants' rooms on the other side
of the baize door. They smelt damp, and in Amy's room the
rain, seeping in through the flat roof above it, had brought a
large piece of plaster down.

'How Mrs. Ravensbourne and her nephew must hate the
child!' Catherine thought as she got with a shiver between the
icy sheets under one threadbare blanket, and she no longer
wondered that her predecessors had not stayed. There had
been a cold mercilessness about the child's great-aunt that
warned her to walk warily, but she was angrily determined to
stand up to her, and she was equally ready to cross swords with
Amy's father at the first opportunity. She refused to believe
that the man did not know how his child was being treated: he
was probably not only aware of the situation but approved of it.

Mice, scampering in the walls, kept her awake, and the bed,
after the comfort of Grey Ladies, was like iron, so that she
tossed and turned, unable to sleep. Her old home, and Anthony
at Trantam Court, and Mrs. Henry Trantam and Bella next

door, seemed to have receded into another world, a bright and glowing world in which people were kind to small children, and servants hurried to answer bells and anticipated one's wishes before they were uttered. A gentler world, that appeared to be unknown to Number Five, Mecklinburgh Square.

The hours dragged by. She added her travelling rug to the blanket on her bed, but creaking boards began to add their uneasy sounds to the frisking of the mice, and once she sat up in bed with a fast-beating heart as she thought she heard soft footsteps outside her door.

'Is anyone there?' she asked, and the mice stopped their scampering to listen, while a velvety silence settled for a few minutes over her room and the corridor outside. Then a gust of wind caught the blind cord and rattled it against her window and she scolded herself for letting taut nerves get the better of her, lay down again, drew the sheet over her head and fell asleep.

Daylight had only begun to penetrate round the edges of the blind when she was awakened by a hand shaking her shoulder with rough gentleness.

'I'm sorry to wake you, miss,' said Maggie apologetically, 'but it's Missus's orders that Miss Amy has breakfast at seven.'

'Then I must get up.' Catherine pushed the tumbled hair from her face. 'What is the time?'

'Just on six, miss, and a nice, fine morning.' As the maid drew up the blind a pink glow from the rising sun touched the little room with warmth. There were no niceties such as pots of tea and thin bread-and-butter for the governess at Number Five, but Catherine had not expected such attentions. 'There's cold water in the jug on your washstand, miss,' said Maggie, 'and if you will wait a little I'll bring you a can of hot after I've taken Pouncer hers and lighted the spirit lamp for her kettle. She likes her early cup of tea, does Pouncer, and I'll never hear the last of it if I'm late.'

'Don't trouble with hot water for me, Maggie. You've enough to do without that, and I can manage very well in cold. But I would like a can presently for Miss Amy. There doesn't appear to be a bathroom on this floor.'

'There's only one bathroom in the house, miss, and that's next to Miss Edith's dressing-room. The Missus had it put in specially for her.'

'Miss Edith is an invalid, I believe?'

'Yes, miss. Something to do with her heart. She nearly died

of it years ago, and she's been near death once or twice since I've been here. The Missus worries herself sick over her.'

'Poor soul.' Perhaps one could not wonder that the woman was abrupt and difficult and spared little thought for Amy. With a child of her own so delicate she would not have much affection for a little girl whose feet could not stop dancing.

'I'll bring the hot water for Miss Amy as soon as I can,' said Maggie, and grinned broadly from the doorway. 'It was the other way round with Mamzelle. She said it was good for children to wash in cold water—it made them hardy—but she had to use hot water because of her skin!'

'What was the matter with it?'

'Well, it was a bit yellow, but no amount of hot water got it any whiter, as I could see!'

Maggie went away and Catherine got out of bed and went to her window, which looked over the town towards the Downs. Between those smooth green slopes and the sea roofs of all angles and sizes stepped up towards Kemp Town behind its grand white terraces, and a haze of smoke from freshly lighted fires rose from small, crooked chimneys against the cold blue of the March sky.

Catherine washed quickly in the cold water, with the help of a large china footbath: she was accustomed to taking a cold bath in the mornings, and although this piecemeal business might be chilly, it was better than nothing. After she was dressed she made her bed and tidied the room to save Maggie trouble and went next door, to find that a can of hot water with a towel neatly folded round it had been set down in the corridor outside. Amy was awake and waiting for her, an anticipatory gleam in her eyes.

'Good morning,' said Catherine, smiling. 'I didn't think you'd be awake.'

'Of course I'm awake,' said Amy scornfully. 'I always wake early. I heard Maggie go and wake you too. Mamzelle didn't sleep a wink the first night she was here. She said the mice kept her awake. Did you hear them?'

'I did.' Catherine drew up the faded blind. 'But, then, you see, I'm used to mice, because Grey Ladies—that's the house where I used to live—is very old, and not only did we have mice scampering about our attics, but we also had an owl window which was left open all the summer, so that the owls might come in and catch our mice for us.'

'I never heard of an owl window before.' Amy went to the

washstand where Catherine was pouring water from the can into the basin. 'Oh . . . lovely! It's *hot*!'

'Will you wash the easy parts while I do your ears and the back of your neck?' said her new governess. Amy made no objection to this arrangement, and Catherine went on talking cheerfully as she worked: 'We had some bees swarm once in one of our attics. My father had to send for the gamekeeper to catch them for his hives, and they both got stung. Our gamekeeper was very clever with bees, though, and he had some lovely honey every year . . . If I ever go there again I'll bring some back with me for our tea.'

Amy glanced at her quickly over the towel she offered. 'If you ever go back there,' she said with an old-fashioned wisdom, 'you'll never come here again. Whenever anybody goes home from here there's always a reason why they can't come back. Their mother's ill, or their married sister's had another baby . . . I can't think why people will go on having babies. They wouldn't if they knew how it puts other people out! I know if I found a baby anywhere I'd just leave it where it was, nasty little thing. It would be no good bringing it here, would it?'

'Well, if it's any comfort to you, I haven't got a home now to go to,' said Catherine. 'And as my sister isn't married she's not likely to have a baby. Sit down and put your stockings on while I make your bed.'

'Maggie will do that. And some people do all the same.'

'Do what?'

'Have babies when they aren't married. I know because Mrs. Stone's daughter, the one who's a Bad Lot, had one, and she wasn't married.'

'Who is Mrs. Stone?'

'She comes to do the washing. Mr. Stone doesn't do any work because he was kicked by a horse. Maggie says that Mrs. Stone's eldest daughter is lady's maid to a duchess and she won't speak to her sister—the one that's a Bad Lot. But I know I'd rather be a Bad Lot than lady's maid to a duchess, especially if the duchess was like my Great-Aunt Anna!' She stopped pulling on the second stocking to look enquiringly at Catherine. 'Why is it wicked to have a baby if you aren't married and not wicked to have one if you are?'

The amateur governess felt that the conversation was getting beyond her and changed the subject. 'Have you no other relatives besides your Great-Aunt Anna and Lady Ulsborne?'

'Well, there's Uncle Selincourt and my father.'

'Have you no grand-parents living?'

'Great-Aunt Anna says they're all dead, but she may have been telling fibs. She said she'd whip me if I told lies, but she doesn't tell the truth herself. She said once that Edith couldn't walk, and she can. I saw her myself once, walking along this corridor.'

'This corridor? But I thought her rooms were on the first floor?'

'So they are. It was at night, too, and when I told Great-Aunt Anna she said I was dreaming and it was wicked to tell lies.'

Catherine remembered the soft footstep she thought she had heard in the night and felt a chill strike her as she buttoned a grubby white petticoat over the child's flannel one, but she said nothing and began to brush out her hair. It was luxurious and curling once the tangles were out of it, and easy to brush into ringlets round her fingers. 'Which dress do you wear in the mornings?' she asked.

'I've only got two, the grey one I was wearing yesterday and the green one with the black velvet collar. It isn't very pretty, but Great-Aunt Anna's dressmaker made it for me out of one that Cousin Edith didn't like.'

The grey dress was put on, the curls tied back with a black ribbon that had already seen good service, and they climbed the attic stairs to the nursery-schoolroom at the top, where Albert was trying to light the fire with damp sticks, while through the skylight the morning sunshine slanted dustily across the bare floor.

'Albert,' said Catherine, after a glance at the empty room which did not improve on this second sight of it. 'I'm going to send for some things from my old home today—books and cushions, and a tablecloth and some pictures, and perhaps some curtains for that bare window. When the boxes come will you bring them up here for me?'

'Why, of course I will, miss. Mamzelle had some things of her own here, too. She said she wasn't used to living in a garret. But she took them all away with her to France.'

'Thank you, Albert.'

Bowls of porridge were brought up to them a little later by Maggie, with another plate of thinly spread bread-and-butter and a pot of weak tea, and after this breakfast Catherine sat down and wrote to Lady Trantam, asking that certain boxes of hers should be despatched as soon as possible. When it was done she took Amy out with her to buy a penny stamp for it, and to make a few small purchases, and then they went down to the shore.

The tide was out, and a few patches of sand beyond the shingle were warm against the grey of the sea. Far out on the horizon, under a pale blue sky where the clouds had broken, was a line of silver light: maybe, thought Catherine, taking heart, it was an omen for the future.

It was twelve o'clock before they were aware of it, and when she took her charge back to Number Five they found Pouncer waiting for them in the hall.

'Miss Amy and her governess always goes in the back way,' she said. 'Mrs. Ravensbourne's orders — Miss Amy should have told you.'

Catherine stiffened, but she felt a small hand stealing apprehensively into hers and she clasped it encouragingly. 'Very well,' she said cheerfully, 'we'll use the back door in future.'

'You can go up the front stairs now you are here.' The woman looked even more sour and ill-tempered than she had the day before. 'But remember in future, that's all. The mistress don't like children's muddy boots all over the clean floor and wearing out good stair-carpets. The back stairs is the place for them. And mind how you go,' she added warningly, as Catherine and Amy turned towards the stairs. 'Don't you dare to make no sound! Miss Edith had a bad night, and isn't at all well today.'

Catherine took Amy's hand more firmly in hers and they crept up the stairs together, scarcely daring to breathe until the baize door was between them and the floor that was given up to Edith. As they reached the attic rooms Catherine asked what time they had their midday meal, and was told that, 'Dinner is at one, I think, but when Cousin Edith is ill sometimes it's much later.'

She glanced at the watch pinned by its plain gold brooch to her black dress and saw that they had nearly an hour in front of them.

'Let's try and find out what you know,' she said. 'I've an idea that what with poor Mamzelle taking away all your books and those other women walking in and out, you may not have learned very much, but that's something we've got to put right between us. It will take a little while, but we'll be undisturbed up here, and we've got all the time there is, haven't we?'

The child drew a step nearer. 'You said that,' she said in a small, shaken voice, 'as if you *did* mean to stay with me ... for always!'

The indignant young woman of the afternoon before seemed to have vanished with the world from which she had come. 'But of course I mean to stay,' said Catherine gently. 'As long as you want me, my love.'

She stooped to kiss the wistful face raised to hers, and was startlingly rewarded by two thin arms that were flung violently round her neck, almost strangling her. 'Oh, please stay with me!' said Amy. 'Please, please stay!'

The bird was safe now, thought Catherine wryly, the last vestige of mistrust had gone, but she herself was caught instead in a trap from which there would be no escape.

A week later two large boxes arrived from Trantam Court, and with them there came an angry letter from Anthony.

My dearest Kate, he wrote, *Mother handed your letter to me and I hope I have found the things you wanted, although I am completely at sea as to why you want them! You say that Bella has been chosen by Aunt Sarah for her companion—it is just the contrary sort of thing she would do!—and that you have obtained employment in the house next door. You don't say what that 'employment'—a hateful word when applied to you! —happens to be, and it would seem that your 'employer'— again, an odious word!—has neglected to furnish your rooms with ordinary comforts. Your boxes, from their labels, contain curtains, tablecloths, cushions, pictures, children's books and lesson books. Has this 'employer', then, put you to sleep in a bare attic, or is she thinking of starting up a school? Please write and enlighten me at once. I can't say that I approve of your situation, in fact compared with the one I offered you before you left and now offer you again—with my undying love, Kate!—it is an outrageous one, and I will thank you to give your notice in at once and telegraph me when it is done.*

Your distracted Anthony

Lady Trantam also wrote a short letter, but although it expressed a similar disapproval for her 'employment', she appeared to accept the necessity for it far more readily than her son, and Catherine detected a note of satisfaction in her letter.

We are all busy with preparations for dear Anthony's coming of age in May, she wrote, *and after that we go to London for the Diamond Jubilee. I know you will not misunderstand me, my dear, when I say how sorry I shall be not to see you and Bella here, and how much we shall miss you in London. Nobody could regret the events of the past few months more than I have, but it would be unkind to encourage hopes that can never be realized, and I know you are too sensible not to see this as clearly as I do.*

Your sincere friend, Alicia Trantam

Catherine put the letter down with a feeling of anger against her sincere friend, and then set herself firmly to accept the inevitable. Lady Trantam had, after all, only emphasized the gulf that she had known existed between herself and the old life at Grey Ladies.

'It is bad news?' asked Amy anxiously, looking from her grave face to the letter. 'Is it from somebody wanting you to go home?'

Catherine tore the letter up and put the pieces in the fire. 'Don't you remember that I told you I had no home to go to?' she said, smiling at her charge reassuringly. 'I'm here for keeps!'

And when the curtains were up at the window, and cushions softened the hard chairs, and a gay Indian tablecloth covered the table, and Albert put up the pictures on the walls, the shabby attic rooms took on such a pleasant and homely air that Amy's delight more than rewarded her governess for the trouble she had taken.

The books were stacked away on the shelves, their gay covers adding more colour to the room, and after tea Catherine read her favourites aloud, while Amy sat herself down on a cushion at her feet. That evening Miss Whittingham wrote a short note of thanks to Anthony's mother and added a hope that the May festivities might go as well as they hoped, and that the sun would shine for them all. She did not mention Anthony, except to send him her regards, and a request that his mother would thank him for having seen that her boxes were so promptly despatched.

6

The next morning was one of those bright March days when the houses and streets of any seaside town look newly washed and sparkling. The sky was blue, with woolly clouds blowing across it before the wind, which was in the east, and ready to catch old gentlemen's hats and errand boys' caps and send them bowling down the parade. A boisterous rollicking sort of wind, with no respect for anybody, whether it was a lady's skirt, or a servant-girl trying to hold on to her hat, or the cyclists who toiled up the hill towards Rottingdean.

It came round Mecklinburgh Square that morning in a tearing hurry of playfulness, sending last years' leaves scurrying down into the area. At Number Five, Cook opened the door to the butcher's boy and received an apron full of dust as she took in the leg of mutton.

'Albert!' she cried up the area steps. 'Albert! When you've collected all them leaves wash the steps down and stop this dust. And put some pails of water over the pavement when you've finished the front steps. It's blowing enough to choke you.'

Albert swept the leaves into a pile in the gutter, where the wind instantly took hold of them and sent them up in a miniature whirlwind before depositing them in the area of Number Three. Then he fetched his bucket to wash the steps, whistling as he worked, glad to be out in the keen air and the sunshine, and to see what was going on in the square as a change from incarceration behind the barred windows of the scullery.

He had just started on the top step when a lady and gentleman who had been strolling down the square from the direction of the sea stopped in front of the house.

'This must be the one,' said the gentleman. 'Number Five, Mecklinburgh Square.' He raised his voice. 'Perhaps you can tell me, my boy! Does Mrs. Ravensbourne live here?'

Albert looked round from his bucket and nodded. 'She does, sir. Do you want to see her?'

'If you please.'

'Very good, sir. I'll just move my bucket and then if you will come up here I'll open the door to you.'

The visitors ascended the front steps and Albert went down the area and into the kitchen in the basement, where Cook had been joined by Mrs. Ravensbourne, the black alpaca apron tied over her dress and a duster in her gloved hands. The leg of mutton was on the table between them, and by the angry look on Cook's face and the determination on that of her mistress, Albert guessed that the size of the leg was in question, Mrs. Ravensbourne declaring that it was too large and must be sent back, and Cook affirming that it would go to nothing when it was cooked.

'You needn't come down here telling me you've done them steps already,' said Cook directly she saw Albert, glad to vent her rage on a third party. 'Because I know you haven't.'

'No,' said Albert. 'But there's a gentleman and lady come to see the Missus, so I had to stop to let 'em in.'

'What do you mean, let them in?' Mrs. Ravensbourne momentarily forgot the leg of mutton. 'Who are they?'

'The gentleman gave me his card, ma'am, and here it is. His face is as brown as our front door, like as if he's come from furrin' parts.'

'Mr. Chester?' Mrs. Ravensbourne frowned at the card in her hand. 'Never heard of him, but you can go on with the steps, Albert. I will see what they want.' She sailed off to open the door herself, not troubling to take off the apron or to relinquish her duster, so that it was scarcely surprising that her visitors took her for the housekeeper.

'Yes?' she said peremptorily, as they stood staring at her, waiting to be asked inside. 'I am Mrs. Ravensbourne. What do you want with me?'

'I have a message for you, madam,' said Mr. Chester recovering himself. 'I would like to have a word with you in private if I may.'

She looked as if she would like to refuse and said abruptly, 'I don't usually receive visitors unless they are known to me.'

'And I would not dream of troubling you,' replied the gentleman stiffly, 'if it were not important.'

Mrs. Ravensbourne glanced at his card a second time and

then said unwillingly that she would see them for a few minutes.

'Thank you.' The couple followed her into the same dismal little room that had chilled Catherine on her arrival, while Albert made as long a job of his scrubbing of the steps as he could, hoping to witness the outcome of the affair.

Having got her visitors into the most unwelcoming room in her house Mrs. Ravensbourne requested them to state their business and go, as she had a great deal to occupy her time.

'And I'm sure we don't wish to trespass on it.' Mr. Chester's voice was as cold as hers. 'My wife and I have come to see the little girl who lives here under your care.'

'Indeed? Did my nephew tell you to call?'

'No. But we were given your name and address, which we were told was also that of little Amy Ravensbourne.'

'Then I'm sorry you've had so much trouble. I don't allow Amy to see visitors.'

'Isn't that rather extraordinary?'

'Extraordinary or not, this happens to be my house, and I make what rules I like in it.'

Mr. Chester seemed to be too astonished to speak, and his wife put in gently:

'Mrs. Ravensbourne, we have no personal interest in the child. We are here because of a promise I made to a lady we met in South Africa. Her husband had recently bought a farm up in the Matabele country, and the Zulus were so unfriendly that we tried to persuade her to stay with us for a time. But she refused to be left behind, and on the day they left she gave me this little packet, knowing that we were shortly coming home, and asked me to look for little Amy Ravensbourne and give it to her with her love. I promised her I would, and I look on it as a sacred trust, because a fortnight later we heard that she and her husband had been murdered and their farm burnt to the ground. The whole of Cape Colony was ringing with it.'

Mrs. Ravensbourne seemed quite unmoved and only said coldly, 'May I enquire the lady's name?'

'Well, her husband called himself John Blake, but we were told after his death that his real name was John Blake Tempest, and that he had held a commission in the Army at one time.'

'Tempest!' Mrs. Ravensbourne was no longer cold: her eyes were furiously alive, and her voice shook with anger. 'You *dare* to speak that name in my house! ... Take your trumpery parcel and go! ... Go at once!'

'But, Mrs. Ravensbourne . . .' Mrs. Chester looked at her helplessly. 'May we not leave this for the child? . . . The woman who wished her to have it is dead.'

'And do you expect me to be sorry for that? A woman who has brought nothing but shame and disgrace on our family.' She stalked to the door and flung it open. 'Please go. And if you leave that parcel with me it will go on the kitchen fire.'

Mr. Chester picked up the parcel, took his wife's arm and a few minutes later the front door slammed behind them. Albert saw Mrs. Chester stop for a moment and cling to her husband.

'What a dreadful woman!' she said in a trembling voice. 'I've never seen such fury in anybody . . . she was like a mad thing. Poor, dear Mrs. Tempest! What could a lovely creature like her have done to make anybody hate her so dreadfully?'

'Don't upset yourself, my dear! Beautiful women often do make a lot of enemies.' Mr. Chester took her hand and patted it consolingly. 'But I must say if I'd known how unpleasant the lady was I'd have posted the parcel to the little girl and chanced her getting it.'

'Poor little creature!' said his wife compassionately. 'I pity her from the bottom of my heart.'

They walked back towards the sea-front, and the area door opened.

'Albert,' said Cook in a resigned tone, 'when you've done them steps you've to take this leg back to the butcher's and tell him it's too large, and if he can't cut us a smaller one it's to be chops, and scrag at that. And ask him where's the sweetbreads for Miss Edith's lunch. I'm waiting to get them done.'

'Very well. I'll be as quick as I can.' Albert finished the steps, shot the contents of his bucket over the pavement and went off with the leg of mutton to the butcher's.

Mr. Clay was large and stout, and spoke his mind about Mrs. Ravensbourne's thriftiness, pushing his straw hat to the back of his head and wiping his knife on his blue-striped apron.

'That leg,' he told Albert wrathfully, 'was as fine and juicy a leg of Southdown as ever I sold. There's not many legs like that in the whole of Brighton. Hung just right, too. It would eat like butter, and it's a sin and a shame to change it.'

'I know,' said Albert. 'But if it's not changed then it's to be scrag.'

'And scrag it will be!' said Mr. Clay. He snatched the leg from Albert's basket and substituted for it a parcel of bones. Albert reminded him about the sweetbreads, and he added them to the bones with the bitter comment that it was a good thing somebody in that house lived well. Albert walked back slowly to Mecklinburgh Square, dawdling because the morning was so fine and the sea so lively and the shore so full of interest, and he saw Mr. and Mrs. Chester sitting on a seat on the parade with Amy's present wrapped in its brown paper between them. It seemed a shame that she should not have it, and he stopped in front of them and touched his cap.

'If you please, sir,' he said, 'if I'd known that parcel was for Miss Amy I'd have told you it was no good, because the Missus never lets her have nothing if she can help it.'

'Poor little girl!' said Mrs. Chester indignantly, but her husband studied Albert with a mild interest.

'I was thinking, sir,' said Albert eagerly, 'if you'd trust it to me, I'd see as Miss Amy got it.'

'I daresay.' Mr. Chester shook his head. 'But will she be allowed to keep it? That's the thing.'

'Well, she's got a new governess what isn't afraid of nobody. I think she would look after it for her. Miss Whittingham has a way of looking at you as if she's used to having her own way, and she's a very nice young lady.'

'Whittingham? Would she be related to General Whittingham, by any chance? I knew him many years ago, when we were both serving in India, but he wasn't a General then, and he had a great deal more money than I had, so that our roads did not run together for very long.'

'I think Miss Whittingham's father was a General, sir.'

'Indeed? How does she come to be a governess, then, a young lady in that position?'

His wife put her hand on his arm. 'Isn't it enough to know that we can trust the parcel to her, dear? Miss Whittingham's private affairs are no concern of ours.'

'That's very true.' He gave the parcel to Albert. 'I shall be glad if you will give it to your Miss Whittingham, my boy, and tell her that it is for Miss Amy. We don't know why the giver was so anxious that she should have it, but it may have been for an important reason, so I should be obliged if you will do your best with it.'

'She shall have it, sir.' Albert tucked the parcel under the bones and sweetbreads and hurried home, and on arriving at Mecklinburgh Square he transferred the precious object to the coal-cellar until he could find the opportunity to take it upstairs. The result was that when he finally produced Amy's present from the bottom of the schoolroom scuttle on the following morning it was as black as the coals.

'I'm sorry,' he said in reply to the astonished looks of Amy and her governess, 'but it was the only way I could get it to you, miss. They was watching of me like cats downstairs.' He told them about the Chesters' visit and how they had been routed by Mrs. Ravensbourne, and the fate that awaited the parcel if she should find it, and then they heard Maggie calling him and he had to go.

Catherine dusted off the parcel before Amy untied the string and the little girl opened it with great excitement: when one receives no presents even the dullest of packets can take on a magical air, and this one, though puzzling, was not dull.

Inside the paper there was a small, carved sandalwood box, lined with silver and with the initials M.S. and J.B.T. entwined in silver on the lid. A tiny silver key was attached to the handle and when Amy fitted the key into the lock and turned it she would not have really minded if there had been nothing inside it at all. But the contents, which might have disappointed more sophisticated eyes, enchanted her by their mystery and unexpectedness.

First there was a sealed letter addressed to, 'Amy Ravensbourne, to be read by her when she is twenty-one', which made sure that the parcel really was intended for her. Then there were some important-looking documents tied with red ribbon, then six silver bangles and a coral necklace, and finally a little cotton bag of glass beads.

'Isn't it exciting?' Amy examined her treasures with delight. 'May I wear the bangles and the necklace?'

'Better not, darling. Mrs. Ravensbourne might see them and wonder where they came from . . . and these papers may be important. I wouldn't like them to be burnt.' Catherine puzzled over the little box. 'I think I'll lock it away in my trunk, just as it is. It will be safe there until we can find somebody to advise us what to do with it. Perhaps Lady Ulsborne would keep it for you: we'll ask her when we see her again.'

But that might not be for another year, and in the meantime it was safer under lock and key. She put it away in her trunk and slipped the key into her pocket, and then she called Amy and they got ready for their walk.

*   *   *

They had got into the habit of looking for inexpensive extras to lighten the dullness of their afternoon teas, and one afternoon, about a week later, after taking the horse tram as far as Shoreham, Amy and her governess were exploring the lanes for primroses when they came upon a farmhouse where fresh eggs and butter were for sale. It happened to be a day when the farmer's wife had been baking, and when they had purchased their butter and eggs from her she threw in a small crusty loaf for good measure. Catherine had no scruples in accepting it: for a child so bereft of small pleasures as Amy she was prepared to take treats from anyone kind enough to offer them.

It was a fine, fresh afternoon, and they were walking home along the promenade after the tram had put them down when Catherine heard her name called, and looking round she saw Mrs. Trantam's carriage stopping beside her, with Mrs. Trantam and Bella seated in it.

'Where have you been all this time?' asked Bella reproachfully, glancing at Amy with a fleeting curiosity. 'I've watched for you in the square early and late, but the front door next to ours never seems to open except when Mrs. Ravensbourne and her daughter go for a drive, and you don't appear at all. Is Number Five a dungeon? I began to think we'd never set eyes on you again!'

'That's only because Mrs. Ravensbourne likes us to come and go by the back entrance.' Catherine glanced about her. A gentleman was sitting with his back to them a few yards away, absorbed in his newspaper, and nobody else was in ear-shot. She gave Amy a gentle push forward. 'Amy dear, this is Mrs. Trantam, who lives next door to us, and this is my sister, Bella.'

The child said how d'you do shyly and Mrs. Trantam said in a dissatisfied voice, 'I'd hoped you would be allowed to bring Amy in to tea with me, but when I sent a note to Mrs. Ravensbourne asking her permission it was curtly refused.'

'I'm afraid visitors and visiting are not encouraged at Number Five.'

'What have you got in that basket on your arm, Amy?' asked Bella, smiling. 'Primroses?'

'Only a few on top. They aren't quite out yet.' The child lifted the flowers to show her. 'Underneath there are some eggs and butter, and a lovely new loaf for our tea. The farmer's wife gave it to us. We didn't have to buy it.'

'I have bought a little saucepan,' said Catherine quickly. 'And we boil eggs—and sometimes shrimps when we can get them from the fishermen. It's great fun. I have the spirit lamp we used in Italy. Do you remember, Bella, how Aunt Emily would never let us go without our afternoon tea?'

'Lady Ulsborne said that the food at Number Five was bad,' said Mrs. Trantam, frowning. 'But she didn't say you would be starved. *Are* you starved, Miss Whittingham?'

Catherine glanced at her charge. 'Amy, my love,' she said. 'I can see the little goat carriage coming this way . . . Run and ask the boy leading it how much he charges for a ride in it, and if he will be out tomorrow morning. I promised you a treat for getting all your sums right this morning.' As Amy sped away down the parade she went on quickly: 'Mrs. Ravensbourne is thrifty, but for all we know she may wish to save her nephew's money. But I always see that Amy has sufficient, and I think already she is a little fatter than when I came. Her face certainly has more colour in it.'

'And you are considerably thinner,' said Bella resentfully. 'Are there any servants to wait on you, Kate?'

'There's Maggie and there's Albert,' said Catherine, smiling, and as Amy came running back with the information she wanted she changed the subject. 'There's no need to ask how you are, Bella! You look radiant.'

The new white blouse under the black jacket and the white wing in the hat against the bright hair added something to Bella's looks, and Catherine's eyes went to Mrs. Trantam as she said gratefully, 'We have a lot for which to thank you there, I am sure.'

'Oh dear no, I'm not the cause for Isabella's pink cheeks, I assure you!' Mrs. Trantam patted her young companion's hand affectionately. 'My nephew and his sisters are staying with us for a few weeks, and they have been monopolizing your sister, taking her to concerts in the evenings and for walks in the morning. They are an excellent tonic for her, and provide the nonsense that she misses in my more sober friends.'

'And look at what they brought with them!' added Bella, holding up Glossy for her sister to see. 'The poor little fellow nearly went mad when he saw me again. Mrs. Trantam says I may keep him here: isn't it kind of her?'

'He's such a good little dog that he is no trouble,' said Mrs. Trantam placidly, and Catherine wondered if Anthony had once told her that his aunt would never tolerate a dog in her house, or if she had dreamed it. 'And when Isabella has not the time to exercise him Hannah is pleased to take him out. He is becoming very spoiled, though, and Anthony says he will get too fat unless he is kept out of the kitchen.'

'Anthony always said that we overfed him.' Catherine packed the eggs more securely in Amy's basket under the primroses.

'Anthony wanted to call on you,' said Bella quickly. 'But we didn't think you would have been allowed to see him if he did.'

'That's very true. A dragon by the name of Pouncer guards the door day and night!' Catherine forced a laugh. 'How are the two girls?'

'Dulcie has had a bad cold, which is why they are here so early in the year. The doctor recommended sea-air.'

'Dulcie was never very strong. In fact, when you were both small there was a kind of rivalry between you as to which should take the most cod-liver oil in a winter!' Catherine took Amy's hand. 'Come, child, we must be going, or we shall never get that egg boiled for your tea!'

They said goodbye and the carriage went on, leaving her to walk back to Mecklinburgh Square with Amy alone.

7

William Ravensbourne put away his newspaper, took a letter from his pocket and read it through with a puzzled air, and then, having digested its contents for a second time, he got up from his seat on the parade and followed Miss Whittingham and her charge at a leisurely pace. Mecklinburgh Square was empty when he reached it, and as Pouncer opened the door he fancied she looked disconcerted to see him there.

'Why, we thought you was in Yorkshire, Mr. William,' she said.

'And, instead, I am here.' He stepped into the dark hall: as usual the floors were polished to a point of danger to life and limb, there was not a speck of dust on the furniture, and the stair-carpet had been brushed until he was afraid to tread on it. Mrs. Ravensbourne had always been houseproud to the exclusion of comfort, and for the first time he tried to see her house through the eyes of a stranger, or as it might appear, for example, to a young woman accustomed to wealth, who would scarcely notice if stair-carpets were muddied because there was always somebody whose work it was to brush them clean again.

The thought brought with it a sense of uneasiness that stayed with him as he followed Pouncer up to the large drawing-room on the first floor. Edith was sitting alone on a sofa drawn up to the fire, listlessly embroidering a cushion cover, but her pale face lighted up when she saw him and she raised her cheek for his kiss.

'My dear William! Mother didn't think you'd be back again for months. What have you come to see her about?'

'Some private business. And why aren't you out in the carriage on this lovely afternoon, instead of being cooped up here in this hothouse? No wonder you're an invalid, Edith. I couldn't endure that fire and those closed windows for a moment.'

'I had a sore throat when I woke this morning,' complained his cousin. 'Mother sent for the doctor and he said I was to keep warm today.' She stole a sly glance at him. 'Did you know that Mary is dead?'

'Yes.' He strolled to the window and stood there, staring down at the gardens.

'I'm *glad*!' said Edith softly. 'She was murdered by some natives out in Africa ... I hope they tortured her before they killed her.'

'Edith!' He spoke sharply. 'That's not the way to speak of her now, whatever she did to you in the past.'

'You always worshipped her, didn't you, Will? You could forgive her anything ... but I'm not like you. They thought themselves so grand, Helen and Mary Selincourt, and they hadn't a penny piece between them. Even their ball-dresses were made by their village dressmaker!'

'What of it? It isn't a crime to be poor, and it's all finished and done with now. For God's sake let's forget if we can!' His voice was suddenly weary and she laughed maliciously.

'Will you be able to forget Mary? I know I shan't, as long as that miserable child of hers is alive ... I saw her walking along the parade with her new governess yesterday. Miss Whittingham reminds me of Mary. She has that same proud air with her, as if she were a queen and the rest of us just dirt under her feet.'

'I think you are doing her an injustice,' said William quietly, but before they could discuss Catherine further the door opened and Mrs. Ravensbourne came into the room.

'Pouncer said you want to speak to me, William,' she said. 'But if you have come on the same errand as before you could have kept away, because I haven't changed my mind.'

'I didn't think you would in so short a time. I have come to see you on something entirely different, Aunt Anna—a private matter.'

She glanced at his face and said abruptly: 'You had better come into my little sitting-room, then. Edith looks flushed. I'm afraid she is a bit feverish today.'

'No, I'm not.' The girl's over-bright eyes met her mother's with defiance. 'Mother, Will knows about Mary!'

'Well, I suppose he would know about her.' Mrs. Ravensbourne spoke composedly. 'After all, he was still her husband. Whatever she might have done, he never disgraced our family by divorcing her.' She went to the sofa and put her hand on her daughter's forehead. 'You are very warm, darling . . . Try not to excite yourself. It is so bad for you. Sit and rest while I talk to William, and then perhaps he will stay and have some tea with us. I know Cook has made some of his favourite scones.' She took away the embroidery and folded it, and Edith lay back on the sofa and closed her eyes.

They left her to sleep and crossed the corridor to a little room above the mews that Mrs. Ravensbourne used as a writing-room, and as the door closed on them William said abruptly, 'I hope Miss Whittingham is proving satisfactory?'

His aunt stared. 'I'm afraid I don't trouble myself with Amy's governesses, William. This one is a stuck-up piece, but I think she is learning her place, and she is better than the other that Lady Ulsborne found for you—a Frenchwoman, full of grievances and fancied slights.'

'Yes, I had a letter from her the other day.' William spoke quietly. 'In it she expressed some of those grievances very forthrightly, and that is why I am here, because if there is any truth in what she says I feel you should know what has been going on. I know your time and attention must be fully occupied with poor Edith, but I'm afraid you may have a dishonest servant who has been feathering her own nest at the expense of the schoolroom.'

'A dishonest servant in my house?' His aunt stared at him incredulously. 'What do you mean?'

'I know you will find it hard to believe.' He took the letter from his pocket and unfolded it. 'I'll read you what Mademoiselle says, and then you can form your own conclusions. She begins: *It is only because of my deep affection for your little daughter that I have stayed six months in Brighton. I could not stay any longer because my health gave way under the treatment I received.*' He paused. 'Shall I go on?'

'Please do!' Mrs. Ravensbourne gave a tight-lipped smile. 'It is quite astonishing. Does Mademoiselle enlarge upon this "treatment" at all?'

'She does indeed. She says that she and the child were starved, and frozen in the winter, with very little fire in the schoolroom and insufficient blankets on the beds. That Amy was not allowed to learn music or dancing, and that her clothes were more those of a beggar than the child of a gentleman.'

Mrs. Ravensbourne listened in grim silence and then observed that he appeared to have a short memory.

'When Mary left you Amy was a year old, and you told me you intended to put her into an orphanage as you could not bear the sight of her. Lady Ulsborne and her husband were abroad, and I persuaded you to let me have her so that she could be brought up by her own kith and kin. And that in spite of the fact that my own darling Edith was just recovering from a most serious illness! I did not promise to employ French governesses, I'm afraid, but I put Amy into the top floor of my house where she could offend nobody, under the care of a nurse, and you were glad enough to agree to this arrangement. I don't think her nurses complained of being starved, and neither did Lady Ulsborne have any criticism to offer until she came back to England some years later and had a sudden fad that she wanted to adopt Amy. I had no doubt that it was only a passing fancy, as most of her whims are, and I begged you not to give in to her. You took my advice, but now it appears she is ready to make trouble again through this Frenchwoman. I should have thought you had more sense than to listen to any tool of hers.'

He moved restlessly under these reproaches.

'But Mlle Birard happens to be an excellent person with the highest references, Aunt Anna. After I found this letter waiting for me in Yorkshire I wrote at once to her former employers, and I had a letter by return of post, informing me that her integrity could not be doubted.'

'May I ask, then, whose integrity you do doubt?'

'Not yours, Aunt Anna. You know that. But I think you may well have a dishonest servant who is responsible for serving bad meals to the schoolroom and taking for her own any extra blankets you may put out in the winter.'

'Impossible!'

'Well, it may be impossible, but let's have your cook up here and question her. From this letter it looks as if there must be something wrong somewhere.'

'I couldn't possibly suspect Cook of dishonesty and neither could you. She has been with me for years.'

'That is no proof that she is honest. You are too trusting, Aunt Anna.' William's face was fully as determined as his aunt's, and he thought he caught the same disconcerted look in her eyes as he had seen in Pouncer's.

'I trust nobody,' she said coldly. 'I never have. I lock up everything, and I do my own housekeeping. Mademoiselle was always putting her stomach and comfort before everything else. You can't believe a word of any letter she writes. A woman like that is a born trouble-maker wherever she goes.'

'Yet she stayed here six months.'

'Lady Ulsborne engaged her: I did not like to dismiss her, and she happened to have taken an absurd fancy to Amy.' She waited for a comment, and as none came she added, 'I hope you are satisfied now?'

'I'm sorry, but I should still like to see your cook. Not to make any accusations, but simply a few enquiries.'

'Please yourself.' She was resentful and angry. She gave the bell an impatient tug, and when Pouncer came she told her to send Cook upstairs.

Cook came in a flurry, and was puzzled and suspicious when William asked her what dinner had been served in the schoolroom that day. He saw her glance quickly at her mistress before replying.

'Chops, sir. Lovely tender chops, with the best spring cabbage and roast potatoes, and a rice pudding to follow.'

'It might have seemed plain fare to a French mademoiselle, William,' observed Mrs. Ravensbourne maliciously, 'but it's the sort of midday dinner that we English often serve in our nurseries and schoolrooms.'

He frowned. 'That was the meal that was ordered and that

you cooked, I suppose, Cook? Did you see it served in the schoolroom yourself?'

'Oh no, sir. Maggie takes it upstairs.'

'Thank you. You may go. And please have Miss Whittingham and Miss Amy sent to me here.'

'Yes, sir.' Cook departed, smarting under a sense of injury. It was plain that somebody had been making trouble about the schoolroom meals—that French mamzelle, no doubt. She'd always known she would in the end. Hadn't she said time and again that the food sent up to the schoolroom wasn't enough to feed a fly? And hadn't she, Cook, done her best to add to the meals there until the Missus asked so many questions that she was afraid of losing her place? Nobody in her position could risk being dismissed as unreliable over food. But it wasn't fair to blame it on her when everyone knew that the Mistress counted every potato and every slice of bread that went up to the schoolroom.

'Why do you want to see Miss Whittingham?' asked Mrs. Ravensbourne after Cook had gone. 'Don't you believe her?'

'Yes, I do. But it is obvious to me that somebody has been lying and I think we should try to find out who it is.'

In a few minutes Catherine appeared, bringing Amy with her and wondering what was wrong, and then, as she saw Mrs. Ravensbourne's visitor, she stopped short.

'Amy's father, Mr. William Ravensbourne, wants to ask you some questions, Miss Whittingham,' said Amy's great-aunt acidly.

Catherine's eyes went to William Ravensbourne and she waited for him to speak, noticing resentfully that he was regarding her with the impersonal interest that he might have given a bale of his own cloth. The truth was that with her pale, grave face and composed, dignified manner she was so unlike the animated creature he had seen recently on the parade, that he found it hard to believe she was the same young woman. He said abruptly:

'Miss Whittingham, will you please tell me what you had for your midday dinner today?'

He saw her start, and, like Cook's, her eyes went to Mrs. Ravensbourne before she replied quietly, 'Amy had two chops, potatoes and cabbage, followed by rice pudding.'

Mrs. Ravensbourne threw a triumphant glance at her nephew, but he ignored it and persisted, 'You say Amy had this ... did you not have it, too?'

She hesitated, and then she said reluctantly: 'No. I dined off bread and cheese.'

'Why? Don't you like chops?'

'Very much.' The dark eyes held surprised contempt that he should think her faddy over food. 'But when there is only enough for one, and that one a growing child, needing plenty of food, I prefer to dine off bread and cheese.'

'Has this happened before?'

She replied indifferently that it happened most days.

'So it would appear that Mlle Birard was right. Did it never occur to you, Miss Whittingham, to tell Mrs. Ravensbourne what was going on?'

Catherine looked at him thoughtfully. For all this show of indignation she did not think he was ignorant of what went on in his aunt's house. Obviously Mademoiselle had said something that had alarmed him and put him on his guard. She said quietly, 'I did ask Cook soon after I came if we could have larger portions in the schoolroom, but she told me she was acting under orders.'

'Indeed?' His air of astonishment was well done. 'Whose orders, pray?'

'I am afraid I did not ask.'

'I see.' But from the anger in his face it seemed that he saw nothing very clearly, and his next remarks were addressed to his daughter, who was clinging to Catherine's hand as if she were a new-found rock in a shifting world. 'Your Aunt Helen and your cousins are to spend a part of the summer in Brighton,' he told her. 'Lady Ulsborne asked me if I would allow you to see them while they are here, and I said you had my full permission to do so. You would like that, wouldn't you?'

Amy gave a little gasp and shook her head.

'What does that mean?' Her father frowned at her impatiently. 'Yes or no?'

'No,' she said. 'I mean I wouldn't like it at all!'

Mrs. Ravensbourne cut across his surprise with a short laugh. 'Helen appears to have been meddling again,' she said. 'If you had asked me, William, I could have told you that Amy doesn't like her cousins.'

'But I do!' The child's protest was high-pitched and shrill. '*They* don't like me. The last time I went to tea with the Selincourts they asked me why I was dressed like a poor person's child, and they said it must be because my father wasn't a gentleman—'

'Amy! Be silent!' Mrs. Ravensbourne was advancing on her furiously when her nephew stopped her.

'Wait!' he said. 'I would like to hear what Amy said to the young Selincourts in reply to their rudeness.' And then, as she hung her head in silence, scarlet and ashamed of her outburst, he said sharply: 'Well? I'm waiting to hear!'

Amy's lips quivered and her eyes filled, and Catherine stooped swiftly and gathered her into her arms. 'Bella was right,' she thought indignantly. 'The man is just a common tradesman . . . with the manners of his kind.' Aloud she said gently: 'Tell him, darling. Don't be afraid . . . Nobody will hurt you while I am here.'

And from that protecting shelter Amy said in a small, shaken voice: 'I said a person couldn't help their clothes being old and shabby and torn . . . I said a person had to have the clothes that were given to them to wear . . . and I said my father was as fine a gentleman as theirs, and finer.'

William had his back to the light and it was difficult to see the expression on his face, but there was no mistaking the scorn and contempt in Catherine's as she glanced up at him over his daughter's head. 'Have you finished with us now, Mr. Ravensbourne?' she asked coldly. 'May we go?'

'No, you may not.' He felt that somebody, somehow, had put him in the wrong: he did not know how it had been done, and his resentment made him brusque. 'Bring Amy over here to the window, where I can see her.'

They came to the window and Catherine pushed Amy into the light so that no detail of her dress could escape him: its shortness and shabbiness, the faded line where it had been let down and the patch of a different colour in the skirt.

'I hope that dress is kept for the schoolroom,' he said shortly. 'I rather agree with the Selincourts. I have seen a labourer's child better dressed.'

'Anything is good enough for the schoolroom, William,' said his aunt smoothly. 'If I save your money on your child's clothes you should thank me instead of complaining. I'm sure Lady Selincourt spends far more on her back than her husband can afford, but the North saves, and the South spends. Your father always said so.'

But there was a decency in all things, and he recollected that the coat that had been worn over that dress on the parade that afternoon had not been any better.

'You will go through Amy's clothes, Miss Whittingham,' he

said peremptorily, ignoring his aunt's remarks. 'And you will make a list of all she needs for Mrs. Ravensbourne to see and act upon, and I hope the next time I see Amy she will not look such a little ragamuffin.' He stared at his daughter, but she was looking at her great-aunt, and there was something in her small face that made him feel increasingly uncomfortable. It had the same quality of proud acceptance and contemptuous indifference that had been in her governess's face, but it was touched too with fear, and he said harshly: 'I don't know what you meant just now when you told Amy not to be afraid . . . I don't think anybody would ever lay a finger on her while she was in this house, because they would know that if they did they would have me to reckon with . . . You may go now. I have said my say.'

'Thank you.' Catherine left the room with the child and Mrs. Ravensbourne exclaimed:

'There's your fine lady for you! Bread and cheese indeed! I can see her dining off that! The sooner we replace her with some sensible body the better, and you may tell Lady Ulsborne that I prefer governesses who dress and act as such, and know their places, and that I'm not having another foreigner in my house either. They only excel at making mischief!'

'Miss Whittingham will stay until I dismiss her.' He was stiff and unyielding. 'Let us understand each other over that. And please tell your cook to see that the schoolroom meals are adequate in future. I don't want you to save my money and win me a reputation for being so mean that I allow my own daughter to starve.'

'And is this all the gratitude I'm to expect for looking after her for seven years? My cook is dishonest and I am parsimonious because I don't believe in indulgence where children are concerned! *You* were brought up strictly, William, and it has done you no harm.'

'It may not have done me any harm, but my childhood was not happy.' He paused, and then added more gently: 'Aunt Anna, you have been very good in giving Amy a home, and I am grateful to you. But this business has made me think that I should not shelve my responsibilities any longer. The day must come when Amy will have to take her place in my house, and now that . . . Mary is dead . . . the old scandal will be forgotten. She cannot be hidden away like this for ever. She must have her music masters and her dancing classes like any other girl.'

'It was your idea to hide her, not mine!'

'Yes,' he admitted slowly, 'it *was* my idea . . . because I could not bear to have her about me in any place where Mary had been. But now things are different . . . I find I can even pity Mary for her behaviour.'

'Pity her? In heaven's name, what next?'

'There were faults on my side as well as hers—'

She cut him short. 'I've no patience with you when you talk like that. You couldn't possibly be blamed for that wretched business. But, as you say, it is over now, and you are free to marry again.'

'After such a calamitous first marriage I'm not likely to try a second!' He came to her and took her hand. 'I must go now. When you have thought things over I know you will agree that Amy should no longer be punished for the sins of her parents.'

But he wondered, as he made his way down the square, if that punishment had not been more cruel than he had ever intended it to be. He felt that it would be a long time before he would forget Amy's defence of him to her cousins. 'I said my father was as fine a gentleman as theirs . . . and finer.'

The words, so unexpectedly generous, so warmly loyal to their relationship of father and daughter, made him feel meaner than the lowest criminal in the land. Her young governess had every right to view him with contempt: she could not have as much scorn for him as he had for himself . . .

*   *   *

Mrs. Ravensbourne went back to her daughter and found her sitting up on her sofa, staring into the grey ash of the fire. As she took up the poker to stir the ash into life, Edith said, 'William seems to take Mary's death calmly, doesn't he?'

Mrs. Ravensbourne put down the poker and sat down in a low chair beside the fire, turning back her skirt over her black silk petticoat. 'It's a long while now since she left him, my dear. It's only natural that he should begin to forget.'

'He is lucky to be able to forget.' Edith's voice shook and her mother put her hand to her quickly.

'Now, darling, Mary is gone and I don't think it will be long before William has Amy to live with him. He said something about it just now.'

'But you won't let him have her?' Edith's thin hands clawed frantically at her mother's. 'You promised . . .'

'I may have promised a lot of foolish things when you were

so ill, but now you are better you must learn to control yourself. You will never get completely well if you go on like this, Edith my love, and we have to remember that Amy is William's child.'

'But she is Mary's child too, and Mary will never be dead as long as Amy lives. You know that as well as I do . . . That is why you promised . . . what you did.'

'I know, love. But you cannot torture a dead woman through a living child . . . and the sooner William takes his daughter from my house the happier I shall be.'

Mrs. Ravensbourne looked anxiously at her daughter, as if waiting for another outburst, but Edith's lips closed themselves firmly and she did not open them again. She went on staring at the grey ash and the heavy steel poker in the grate with a strangely inscrutable expression, and her mother hoped that she had decided to give in gracefully where she had no option to do otherwise.

8

That night once more Catherine found it hard to get to sleep. The blind made the room airless in the fine, spring weather, and she pulled it up to let the cool night breeze into the room. As she watched the moonlight finding its way across her wall she saw again Bella's smiling face in Mrs. Trantam's carriage, the crisp white blouse under the black jacket and the smart little hat with its white wings and veil.

There was no reason why her sister should not discard some of her mourning for their father: he had been dead for four months, and Bella was young and gay. Catherine guessed that Mrs. Trantam had persuaded her young companion to brighten her clothes, and that soon, acting under the same advice, Bella would replace black with grey, and white would figure more and more in her summer dresses. She looked her best in white.

Catherine was glad that things were turning out so well for her sister, and firmly suppressed any feeling of envy that might attack her when she compared Bella's lot with her own. Had she taken Mr. Jason's advice she and Bella might now be installed in a cottage near their beloved Grey Ladies, living on the charity of their father's friends, and it was only because her proud spirit had rebelled against such a prospect, and as a direct result of her own choice, that she and her sister were now in different worlds.

She dropped off to sleep just before midnight and was awakened by a church clock striking three. The moonlight had shifted now to the wall behind her bed, and as she lay there, suddenly wide awake and listening to the distant clock, once again she thought that stealthier sounds accompanied the scampering of the mice in the walls.

Not only did a board creak, but a positive movement came from the corridor outside: there was the soft hush of a dress being dragged over bare boards, and then a light footstep that hesitated before passing on.

She wondered if Amy had been taken ill, and struck a match to light her candle, and the wick had scarcely taken hold before she heard the child's voice cry out in sudden fright. She called out that she was coming, and thrust her arms into her dressing-gown and her feet into slippers and ran into the little room next door.

Amy was sitting up in bed and shaking with terror.

'I woke up,' she said as Catherine put her arm round her. 'There was a sort of bang on my pillow . . . and then I saw somebody standing beside my bed. The moonlight was shining round my blind and I could see her plain as plain, but I couldn't see her face because she had a shawl over her head . . . I was so frightened . . . I thought she was going to smother me, like the Princes in the Tower we were reading about yesterday . . . and so I called out and she disappeared . . . Don't leave me, will you, Catherine? *Please* don't leave me . . . in case she comes back.' Since she had heard Bella call her sister by her Christian name that morning, Amy had dropped the stiff, 'Miss Whittingham', and Catherine had not objected.

'I won't leave you, darling,' she said. She went out into the corridor with her candle, peering into the darkness beyond its small circle of light. The window that lighted the passage was uncurtained, but nothing moved and not a shadow stirred. She waited another moment and then she went back to the child's room. 'Could it have been Pouncer?' she asked. 'Or Mrs. Ravensbourne?'

Amy shook her head. 'I don't know. I didn't see because of the shawl... I was so frightened that I just screamed out for you.'

Catherine took Amy's dressing-gown off its peg behind the door and put it round her. 'I think you'd better come into my bed for the rest of the night,' she said decidedly.

'Oh, may I? And shall I bring Sal?' Sal was the ancient doll that she still took to bed with her.

'If you like.'

Amy picked up the doll and then gave a startled exclamation. 'Look,' she said, 'her face is all broken!'

'So it is!' Catherine thought she saw the explanation of it all. 'That is what happened, Amy. You lay on her in your sleep and broke her face—that was the bang you heard on your pillow, you know—and just before you woke up you had a bad dream about somebody standing by your bed.'

'You don't think it was a ghost, then?'

'No, of course not, darling. Much more like a nightmare.'

'But can I come into your bed just the same?'

'You may certainly, my love. But we'll leave poor old Sal where she is and stick her together with glue in the morning.'

Amy came gratefully, but long after she had snuggled down beside her and dropped off to sleep Catherine found that she could not dismiss the affair from her own mind quite so easily. There were those faint sounds in the corridor, and when she reached Amy's door it had been open, and she distinctly remembered shutting it as usual after she had said good night.

When Maggie came in the morning she did not seem surprised to find Amy in Catherine's room. 'Had a bad dream, did she?' she said. 'It was that cheese Cook sent up for her supper. I said it would give her nightmares, and it did.'

'I thought I saw somebody standing by my bed,' said Amy.

'Did you now?' Maggie laughed. 'I wonder you didn't feel somebody stamping on your stomach!' But after she went next door to pull up the blind she came back and asked Catherine if she could speak to her for a moment. Her face had lost its smile and she looked more than a little troubled, and Catherine left Amy to start washing and followed her into the child's room. Maggie pointed to the bed.

'Can you tell me how that happened, miss?' she asked.

'Sal's smashed face, do you mean?' asked Catherine. 'Why, I think Amy must have rolled over on the doll in the night and broken it. She always takes Sal to bed with her, you know.'

'I know. But she don't take this as well, does she, miss?' And Maggie picked up a heavy poker from the bed.

'A poker!' Catherine stared at the thing as if it were a snake. 'Where did it come from?'

'Oh, I know where it *came* from, all right,' said Maggie. 'But I don't know how it got here, on Miss Amy's bed, alongside that broken doll!'

'Neither do I,' said Catherine, frowning. She weighed the thing in her hand: it was heavy with a steel head to it, and she felt suddenly afraid.

'Miss Amy always sleeps with her head under the sheet,' said Maggie softly. 'And Sal was wrapped in a shawl with her head on the pillow ... I daresay in the dark it would look like—'

'Don't!' cried Catherine. 'Don't say it, Maggie!' She thrust the poker back at the girl. 'Take it back to ... wherever it came from,' she said in a low voice. 'And we'll say nothing about it ... But I want Albert to move Miss Amy's bed into my room today, if he will be so kind. I don't want her to sleep alone any longer.'

Maggie nodded. 'And while he's at it he can tighten the bolt on your door, miss. It's a bit loose, and there isn't a key in your lock, is there?' She added thoughtfully: 'My mother always says it's best for a person to lock her door at night in a big house like this. You never know who might be prowling round in the dark.' And then she went away downstairs, taking the poker with her, and Catherine went back to Amy, who was delighted to hear that she was to move into her room for good.

But although she talked cheerfully as she buttoned up buttons and tied tapes and brushed out Amy's hair, the fear that had touched Catherine when she saw the poker lying beside the shattered doll seemed to tighten its grip.

It was all very well to say that she had imagined danger where none existed, that this was the year 1897, the year of the old Queen's Jubilee, and elderly ladies did not creep about at night frightening their small great-nieces to death with pokers, however much they might happen to dislike them. The thing she feared was difficult to fight because it was unknown, but of one thing she was certain: hate had inspired the child's nocturnal visitor, just as hate had surrounded her in that house before she came, as an amateur governess, to stand between her and those who, in their hatred, seemed now likely to go to any lengths to do her harm.

*   *   *

After breakfast Catherine made a list of the clothes that Amy needed and handed it to Pouncer, asking her to give it to Mrs. Ravensbourne. The woman said sourly that she did not think her mistress would have time to look at it that day.

'She's fair worried to death over Miss Edith,' she said. 'The poor lamb had one of her bad turns early this morning, and I had to go down and get Albert up to go for the doctor. I wonder you didn't hear the noise we made.'

Was there a watchfulness in the black eyes? Catherine could not be sure. 'I woke up thinking I heard something,' she said quietly. 'And Amy had a bad dream. But being at the back of the house we don't hear much of what goes on downstairs.'

Pouncer muttered something about the back being good enough for some, and bounced off with the list. Catherine did not expect to hear any more about it, and was surprised when after a luncheon that had improved in quantity, if not in quality, Maggie came to tell her that her mistress wanted to see her.

Mrs. Ravensbourne was in her little sitting-room, dressed in fine, navy-blue serge that made her look almost handsome in a hard sort of way. She was standing at the window that overlooked the mews and she did not turn her head as the governess entered the room. Catherine waited, refusing to be provoked: one could forgive the woman much because of the poor invalid daughter to whom she was so utterly devoted. She stood looking about her at the furniture, the big roll-top desk that was more suitable to a counting house than a lady's room, the worn carpet, the heavy green serge curtains, and she was wondering if there was some puritanical streak in Mrs. Ravensbourne that made her almost as neglectful of her own comfort as she was of her great-niece when she found that the lady had finished her study of the mews and was examining herself with as much curiosity as she was examining the room.

'I was watching the groom cleaning my carriage,' she said abruptly. 'He has no idea of how paintwork should be polished. No Southerner has any idea of work—they idle their time away in gossip and staring about them.' She picked up Catherine's list from the desk. 'I've looked at this, Miss Whittingham. It seems to be somewhat formidable.'

'Amy has only two dresses to her name, both very old and faded,' said Catherine quietly. 'Her petticoats and nightdresses are in rags, and she has grown out of her one pair of boots.'

'You make this sound a serious indictment!' Mrs. Ravensbourne smiled ironically. 'Who is to blame for it, I wonder?'

'I am not presuming to blame anybody.' Catherine's eyes met the others calmly. 'I was asked to furnish a list of the clothes that are needed, and I have done so.'

The older woman unbent a little. 'I know that, Miss Whittingham, and I will see that the child has what is necessary.' She folded the list and put it back in the desk. 'My daughter was taken ill in the night, so that I cannot do anything today, but directly I feel that it is safe to leave the house I will order the carriage and go to the shops and my dressmaker. I will have all materials sent to her, so that you may take Amy to her house to be measured and fitted.'

Catherine thanked her and said that Amy would be delighted, and was turning to the door when she was called back.

'Pouncer tells me that you have had Amy's bed moved into your room.' Mrs. Ravensbourne's voice had more curiosity than annoyance in it. 'Before you go I would like to know why you have had this done without asking my permission?' Was there a touch of apprehension under the question? Again Catherine could not be sure.

'She had a bad dream,' she said. 'And I thought it was probably because she was nervous of sleeping alone. She is a highly strung child and for a time at least she should have company at night.'

'You are quite right.' Amy's great-aunt was unusually eager to agree with her. 'When my poor little Edith was that age she suffered in much the same way . . . she used to walk in her sleep . . . and on rare occasions she still does!' She waited for a comment, or perhaps an exclamation, but Catherine did not oblige her.

'I'm sorry Miss Ravensbourne is not well today,' she said. 'It must be very worrying for you.' And then she went away, pleased to be able to tell Amy that she was to have some new clothes.

Their pleasure was short-lived. A few days later some boxes of clumsy-looking boots arrived, from which Amy was required to make a selection.

'But these are so heavy!' She slipped her slim feet into them in dismay. 'They are like the boots that Albert wears . . . and they are *much* too big!'

And on the following day a further disappointment waited for them, when, in response to a note sent up to the schoolroom, they visited the neat little terrace of villas where the dressmaker, Mrs. Westcott, lived.

A small general servant showed them into the front room which was the fitting-room, and her mistress came to them there, dressed in a black dress with a white apron over it, a velvet pincushion hanging from her waist and a tape-measure round her neck. She was a nice sensible body, with a pair of shrewd eyes behind her steel-rimmed spectacles.

She studied Catherine's well-cut coat and skirt appreciatively as she took Amy's measurements, and remarked that everyone felt like having new dresses in this bright warm weather.

Some parcels stood on the table in the window and these she opened, saying that they were the materials Mrs. Ravensbourne had ordered, and Catherine and her small charge stared at the contents in silence.

The calico would have been dear at fourpence a yard, the brown serge, of the cheapest rough-and-ready variety, might have cost tenpence, while the alpaca was an ugly shade of slate-grey, quite unsuitable for a child's dress.

'That brown is the same colour that the children from the charity school wear,' said Amy, her lips quivering a little. The Admiral Blake Orphanage occupied the seats in front of them in church. 'Why should my coat be like theirs? I'm not a charity child, am I, Catherine?'

'Of course not.' Catherine's voice was warm with indignation, and she could see that Mrs. Westcott was as put out over the affair as she was, although she tried to soften Amy's disappointment by saying that no style had been selected, and that a lot could be done with ugly material if the cut of a coat was pretty, and if dresses had fine workmanship in them.

'Yes,' said Catherine thoughtfully, the light of battle in her eye. 'I see what you mean . . . Coloured smocking and white lawn collars and cuffs and a neat belt in a contrasting colour would make something even of this alpaca . . . And a velvet collar to the coat perhaps, of a slightly darker brown, and some pretty buttons.' Her eyes met the dressmaker's and Mrs. Westcott nodded.

'Little pitchers have long ears,' she remarked, apropos of

nothing. 'But it always strikes me as sad . . . and strange . . . when a man visits his personal tragedy on a child.'

'Tragedy?' repeated Catherine, frowning.

'Yes,' said Mrs. Westcott emphatically. 'Tragedy . . . I could tell you some things that would surprise you, Miss Whittingham. Not that I'm one to listen to gossip, mind you. But there's an old lady living in this street who used to be nurse to two young ladies in a titled family, from the time they were babies to the day they married. She knows a great deal about certain people connected with those young ladies . . . people not living very far from here.' She pursed her lips and sighed. 'Ah well, it takes all sorts to make a world, as they say.'

'Am I to have no best dress?' asked Amy from the table where the materials were spread out.

'There is nothing for one, my dear,' said Mrs. Westcott sympathetically. 'I wish there were. I'd enjoy making you a pretty muslin dress for the summer.'

'But there are some dresses in my boxes that I shall never wear again!' cried Catherine. 'And there is one very pretty pink muslin among them. If I unpicked it for you, Mrs. Westcott, do you think you could make it up into a party dress for Amy?'

'I would enjoy doing it,' said the dressmaker. 'But you must allow me to unpick it for you, Miss Whittingham, if I may. I fancy it will have been made by a London dressmaker, and the work of such people is an education in itself.'

Catherine admitted that the dress in question had come from Wörth. 'It was made the summer before he died, and it has always been my favourite dress.' She gave a rueful little smile. 'I was encouraged to have expensive tastes!'

'I could tell the moment I saw you that you had been accustomed to good clothes. It isn't only the dresses, it's the way they are worn, if I may say so. Anyone can tell at a glance. I will fetch the dress when I have finished these things for Miss Amy.'

'But don't charge Mrs. Ravensbourne with the making of it,' said Catherine quickly. 'Amy's party dress shall be paid for out of my pocket. And I will hunt out some white muslin, too, for pinafores. We'll make them together, Amy and I, and they shall be frilled and embroidered, with fancy pockets and tiny tucks . . . the loveliest pinafores that anybody could possibly want!'

But as they made their way home her puzzled mind dwelt

upon the cheap and ugly materials, and the clumsy boots that would raise blisters on Amy's feet however well the toes were stuffed with cotton wool, and would certainly spoil the look of any dress she wore with them, and she wondered if Mrs. Ravensbourne alone were to blame for the selection of these things, or whether, in spite of his peremptory orders to herself, William Ravensbourne had given his aunt so little to spend on his daughter's clothes that she had been left with no choice.

Her thoughts were busy following these trends when they were suddenly interrupted by the barking of a dog, and a familiar voice that said gladly: 'Yes, you are right, Bella! It *is* Catherine! . . . Down, Glossy, you bad fellow!' And there in front of her, barring her path, was Anthony, smiling down at her with his old warm delight, and with him his two sisters and Bella, holding on to Glossy's lead with one hand and her hat with the other.

The white wings and veil had been augmented today with a ruching of white ribbon under the brim of the hat, and the black coat and skirt had been replaced by a pale and lovely grey: Bella's mourning was rapidly taking on a lighter tone, and in her own unrelieved black Catherine felt like an unwelcome guest at a party.

'I have looked for you every day,' Anthony told her, his face becoming graver as he examined hers. 'I've walked the parade from end to end in the hope of finding you. Are you quite well, Kate? You look so pale.'

'I am quite well, thank you, Anthony.' She smiled at the girls and avoided his eye: he had been so close to her in the old days that he could almost read her thoughts, and she did not want her thoughts read just then.

Amy's attention being taken up with Glossy and his owner, Anthony walked on a little way with Catherine. 'I still can't think what induced Aunt Sarah to choose Bella instead of you,' he said in a vexed tone.

'Oh, but I can, very well!' She dismissed his concern for her lightly. 'Our temperaments would not have suited at all—we are both too fond of having our own way. Bella is exactly right for Mrs. Trantam—tractable where I am rebellious, sweet where I am sour, generous where I am mean.'

'There never was and never will be any meanness in you!' He spoke hotly, and unwilling to provoke a further outburst she stopped and called to Amy that it was time they went home.

'At least tell me if there is anything I can do for you?' he said as the little girl came running after them.

She hesitated, and then she glanced at Amy's feet, and he saw the old mischievous light flash in her eyes as she laughed.

'You can write home to your mother and ask her if she has by her any parcels of Dulcie's outgrown footwear—boots or slippers, anything will do—from the time when she was Amy's age. If she has any such things and will have them made up in a parcel and sent to me I will receive them with far more gratitude than she would have from the most deserving charity in the world.'

'But . . .' He stared in bewilderment at Amy's shabby boots. 'Doesn't Ravensbourne buy clothes for his daughter?'

'Oh yes,' said Catherine. 'He buys her clothes . . . but he appears to think that her feet are the size of those rowing-boats down there on the shingle! It will be years before she grows into the boots he has provided for her!'

Anthony promised to write to Lady Trantam, and they parted, but Amy's bootlace had come undone, and as Catherine stopped by a seat to tie it for her, the girls' voices came back to her on the breeze of that bright spring day.

'I wouldn't have known Catherine,' Dulcie said. 'She looks so much older!'

'It's being a governess,' said Alice. 'All governesses look thin and careworn. Poor Catherine! I wouldn't be in her shoes for the world.'

Catherine waited to hear Bella rush in to her defence, but she waited in vain. As her fingers fumbled with Amy's lace she heard her sister say: 'I wish you'd stop staring after poor Kate, Anthony, and give me your arm. I'm utterly exhausted with all this walking . . . and so is poor Glossy. It's time we went home to tea.'

9

April moved towards May, and now the short, fashionable Easter season for Brighton's visitors was drawing to a close. During these days Catherine would not have been human if her thoughts had not gone back painfully to May at Grey Ladies, with the tall beech trees coming into leaf, and the tender green of the hedges in the lanes and the cuckoo calling his first gay notes over the park.

She watched for her sister and her friends when she was on the beach with Amy, and if she caught sight of a small black dog on the parade she would hurry her way out of sight. She had no desire to be pitied by Bella's friends, and there was no room in her life now for Anthony's persuasive tongue.

One day, however, when she was walking on West Pier with Amy she heard light footsteps running behind her, and the next moment Bella caught up with her.

'There you are, Kate!' Her sister was smiling and excited. 'I thought it was you, so I left Glossy with Dulcie and I ran to catch you up, because I've been looking for you everywhere. I've got some wonderful news!'

Catherine glanced at the two Trantam girls and Glossy, but they made no attempt to join them and were evidently only waiting until she had finished talking to her sister. 'Well,' she said, smiling down at the pretty, flushed face, 'and now you *have* found me and here I am!' She noticed that the black hat had been discarded for a dove-grey, and she fully expected that the next time she saw Bella the grey would be trimmed with lavender ribbons. 'What is the great piece of news, darling?'

'I'm going to Trantam Court for Anthony's coming-of-age! Aunt Sarah is taking me!'

'Aunt Sarah, Bella?'

'I mean, Mrs. Trantam.' Bella looked a little self-conscious. 'She asked me to call her that, because you see Dulcie and Alice and Anthony all do it, and it sounds stiff and unfriendly if I persist in saying "Mrs. Trantam" all the time!' And then, while her sister digested this in silence, she hurried on: 'Lady Trantam wrote me such a charming letter, saying how pleased they would be to welcome me there . . . Oh, and she sent her regards to you, Catherine!'

'Thank you.' Catherine's tones were dry. She did not wonder that Lady Trantam was ready to welcome this radiant young creature as the current favourite of a very rich woman. Anthony's mother had always liked to keep money in the family. She asked quietly, 'When do you go?'

'Next week. I have been ordering some new dresses. My ball-dress is of white satin . . . Aunt Sarah said it would be in perfectly good taste if I wore white, and she is lending me her amethysts—the necklace and bracelets—and I am to wear violets in my hair.'

'And you will look very beautiful, I'm sure,' said Catherine tenderly. 'You will have to write and tell me all about it.' And then a shower blew up, whipping the surface of the sea and sending them running for shelter, and when it had passed the two Trantam girls came up with Glossy and took Bella away.

A few evenings later Albert brought Catherine a note that had been given him by a gentleman in the mews, and it only needed a glance at the scrawling handwriting to tell her that it was from Anthony. He had never had a good fist. She put it aside, and read it later on after Amy was in bed.

My dearest Kate, he wrote,

We are leaving Brighton in two days' time and I must see you again before I go. Will you bring Amy to the toyshop in King's Road tomorrow morning at ten o'clock? I will be waiting for you there. Please, Kate, spare me a few minutes! It's all I ask.

Your still devoted Anthony

She put down the letter with a mixture of feelings, in which pleasure because he had not forgotten her was mingled with grief because his world was closed to her. Her first instinct was to ignore his request, but the hastily written words teased her throughout the night, and she couldn't help remembering the warm comradeship that had existed between them all their lives. She found it difficult not to envy her younger sister for her beauty and gaiety, and her air of charming helplessness that made people like Anthony's wealthy aunt wish to cherish and protect her. Nobody would ever want to cherish or protect the elder Miss Whittingham: she could well look after herself.

Nevertheless the following morning found her outside the toyshop with Amy dancing about beside her as she gazed with rapture at the goods displayed in the bow-fronted window, and Anthony was waiting there with a smiling impatience equal to Amy's. He took five shillings from his pocket and gave it to the child, telling her to go and spend it on what she liked, and as she sped away into the dark interior of the shop he said:

'Catherine, I had to see you. Your thin face and great dark eyes have haunted me . . . I want you to come with us tomorrow.'

'Now how can I do that?' But her heart lifted, because this was the old Anthony speaking, staunch and comforting in a lonely world. 'What would become of Amy?'

'Hang Amy! You didn't know of her existence a couple of months ago. Let Ravensbourne look elsewhere for a governess, Kate. Your father would have been horrified at such employment for his elder daughter.'

'As your mother is?' she reminded him gently.

'And rightly so!' He took her hand. 'My dearest, lovely, Kate, you've got to come home with me because I want to introduce you to everybody as my future wife. You don't know how I've missed you—your sympathy, your advice, your help . . . I'm lost without you, and I won't endure it any longer. Pride is all very well in its place, but yours is unnecessary. I love you, and I want to marry you, and nothing that anybody can say will alter it. My mind is made up.'

She tried to release her hand. 'But even if it were possible to do as you say I can't leave Amy now. I've promised her that I will stay as long as she needs me, and I've never broken my word to anybody in my life. You know I haven't, Anthony.'

'That's sheer nonsense. She's only a child, and there are scores of governesses about.'

'But none would be *me*. I shall never forget my first sight of her in that attic room—her friendlessness and loneliness. I can't betray the trust she has learned to put in me. She had so little love until I came.'

'Children soon forget. My sisters used to cry their eyes out when a favourite governess left, but they got over it before the next one arrived. You're making a mountain out of a molehill, Kate. Can't you get it into your head that I want to marry you? You could not tell me seriously that you'd rather stay in Brighton teaching the Ravensbourne child her A B C? You said yourself that you were only an amateur governess, Kate!'

'I may be an amateur, and I may not want to stay in Brighton. One's duty is seldom attractive,' said Catherine, slowly. The smile left her eyes and he had a feeling that she was deliberately erecting a barrier between them. 'But I'd rather bring happiness to little Amy than a great deal of unhappiness to you . . . and others . . . who have always been my dear friends.' Her voice broke a little in spite of her efforts at controlling it, and he took a firmer grip of her hand, hoping that she was weakening, when Amy ran out of the shop.

'There are two dolls, Catherine!' she cried excitedly. 'I don't know which to choose. They're both so lovely! Will you come and help me?'

'Of course I will, my love.'

Anthony dropped her hand with an angry exclamation and she went into the shop. It took some minutes to choose the doll: when they came out again he was gone, and Catherine was glad of it. She felt too tired and spent to argue with him any more.

The days went by and Number Three Mecklinburgh Square was empty of all but the servants. The drawing-room was in dust-sheets, the chandeliers encased in muslin, and Catherine had a feeling of personal loss each time she looked at the shuttered windows. Although she had seen little of her sister, at least it had been comforting to know that she was there if she was wanted. By the time Bella's first letter arrived she seemed to have been away for months, although it was only ten days since Mrs. Trantam left.

The letter was ecstatic, however, and Catherine was spared nothing of the preparations for the great day, from the Chinese lanterns that were to be hung in the trees, to the coloured fairy-lights, spelling out Anthony's initials and the date over the entrance gates. There were to be bonfires, and a tenants' dinner and ball in a big marquee in the park, while the ball planned for Anthony's friends and relatives in the ballroom at the Court was to be the biggest and most magnificent the country had seen for a long time.

And in the meantime, until the day dawned, Bella was bicycling about the countryside and finding it great fun.

You know Father would never allow us to bicycle, she wrote. *He thought it vulgar, poor darling. But Aunt Sarah gave Dulcie and me bicycles, because she thinks it is such good exercise, and Anthony taught us to ride—he said I picked it up very quickly. Dulcie wasn't nearly so quick—she kept falling off! But we are so proficient now, that yesterday afternoon we rode over to Grey Ladies with Anthony to see what the old place looked like. I was sorry we went there afterwards, because it is so sad and neglected, Kate. I do wish somebody would buy it. The lawns are hayfields, and our lovely roses scarcely to be seen above it. It took a home-made concert here last evening to make me forget our poor old home. I shan't ride that way again!*

Catherine could see the bright faces gathered round the piano in the drawing-room at Trantam Court: Alice with her violin, Dulcie at her guitar and Bella at the piano, with Anthony's fine tenor voice singing the ballads they sang together at Grey Ladies: 'Comin' thro' the Rye', and 'She is far from the Land', and 'Drink to me Only'. If it had not been for her own troublesome conscience she could have been there with them, as Anthony's future wife.

Here in Brighton there was only Amy's single-minded devotion to reward her for her sacrifice, and it was something to hold fast to when Bella's second letter arrived after the ball. Her white satin had been much admired, she told her sister, and she had carried a bouquet of white roses and her white lace fan.

Several people asked after you, Kate, but I said you were staying with friends. I thought they might not understand if I said you were a governess—even an amateur one! And now for another piece of news: Aunt Sarah and I are going to London with the others for the Jubilee next month. The Trantams have seats on the stand directly opposite St. Paul's, where they will see the Queen's arrival and everything, and as two of their friends have fallen out of the party, Aunt Sarah and I are to take their places. Isn't it fun? I'm so excited ...

Only one sentence in the letter had the power to wound and

hurt: *I said you were staying with friends* . . . Catherine put away the letter and wondered how long it would be before Bella would be ashamed of her sister.

*   *   *

At the end of May Lady Ulsborne came back to Brighton with her children. Sir Richard had taken a house for his family in Brunswick Square, and after they had been there a couple of days Helen screwed up her courage and went to call on Mrs. Ravensbourne. She was shown into the familiar cold little room downstairs, and after enquiring after Edith with a sweetness that did not melt Mrs. Ravensbourne's icy manner in the least, she came to the object of her visit.

'Our eldest girl will be nine years old on Sunday, and it would give us great pleasure if Amy could have tea with us that afternoon. I know you don't approve of her making social visits, but as she has not seen them for two years, having tea with her cousins is not likely to turn her into a butterfly!' She added quickly before the older woman could refuse, 'William said he would like Amy to see a great deal of the children while they are here.'

Mrs. Ravensbourne stared contemptuously at her visitor.

'If William has given his permission,' she said coldly, 'I cannot see what it has to do with me. I will tell Miss Whittingham to take Amy to your house on Sunday afternoon — I think you said it was in Brunswick Square?'

'Yes. Number Twenty.'

'I am surprised that Sir Richard did not select a more fashionable quarter for his family. Brunswick Square has gone down a lot lately: houses there that used to fetch as much as thirty or forty guineas a week in the season are now to be let, I understand, at five for the whole summer.'

'That was why Dick chose it.' Lady Ulsborne was not at all ashamed of her husband's lack of taste. 'He says the air is as good in Brunswick Square as in any other part of Brighton, and we have not come here to be fashionable. The children all had whooping cough in February and our doctor recommended Brighton air for their chests. I shall stay with them until I join Dick for the Jubilee in London, and after that they will be here for the rest of the summer with their nurses and our governess, Miss Mattison.' She got up to go. 'I am glad Edith is a little better.'

'She is as well as she ever will be. You are fortunate to have healthy children.'

'I know.' Helen's voice was suddenly warm with sympathy. 'It must be a great grief to you that poor Edith is so delicate.'

Her pity was thrown back in her face: Mrs. Ravensbourne wanted none from Mary's sister. 'Miss Whittingham will call for Amy at six o'clock.'

'Oh, but I hope Miss Whittingham will stay and have tea with the children, too. Miss Mattison will be there to keep her company, you know.'

And as Lady Ulsborne flitted away to her carriage Mrs. Ravensbourne permitted herself a grim smile of satisfaction. It would do the stuck-up Miss Whittingham no harm to sit down with another governess: it might humble her pride, in fact, and teach her the position in which she stood in the eyes of Lady Ulsborne's world.

She told her of the invitation and Catherine was delighted for her charge. The muslin dress was finished and sent home, a pair of neat black shoes had been discovered to fit in the bundle sent from Trantam Court and Mrs. Westcott had made a muslin sun-bonnet out of what remained of Catherine's dress. She felt that this time Amy would not be ashamed to appear among her cousins, and when she begged to be allowed to wear the bangles and the necklace from the sandalwood box that Sunday she hesitated only a moment before giving permission. The bangles fitted Amy's slight wrists very well, and the corals made a lovely finish to the pink muslin dress.

'You may wear them for this afternoon, darling,' she said. 'No one in this house will see them, because we will go and come by the back way as usual.'

She put the sandalwood box back in the trunk and was about to close the lid when she caught sight of a grey cashmere dress, packed away in tissue paper in the tray. Outside the sun was shining, and the day was too beautiful for mourning, and acting on a sudden impulse she changed quickly into the dress, Amy helping to fasten the hooks and eyes up the back.

'You look much nicer!' she said. 'I'm glad you're going to wear a pretty dress too, Catherine!'

They crept down the back stairs like conspirators, holding their breath, Catherine trying to suppress Amy's giggles as they went. She did not wish to bring Pouncer upon them, or, for that matter, Cook, who was anybody's toady.

They reached the mews unseen and walked away quickly up

the road to the front, and as usual freedom met them in the fresh breeze and the cry of the gulls. The sun was warm on their faces, and as Amy danced along holding fast to Catherine's hand, she found her spirits rising to meet the happiness of the child.

The birthday tea had been set out in the dining-room of the house in Brunswick Square: a large cake was in the middle of the big table, and around it were so many dishes with a variety of good things to eat that Catherine trembled for her charge, fearing she would make herself ill.

But Amy, conscious that her new dress was as pretty as any of her cousins', was far too interested in them to trouble herself about what she ate. The young Selincourts were there and she watched and listened, her eyes round with wonder as they exchanged family jokes with the three older Ulsbornes across the table, the Ulsborne baby being too young to do anything more than blow bubbles through handfuls of sponge cake. After tea the children played cricket in the square under the direction of the two elder Selincourt boys, who kept the score and bowled and batted and caught the younger ones out and sent them to field with ruthless efficiency, and in the middle of it Lady Ulsborne came out and called to Catherine to come and sit beside her in the shade of some trees.

'The Selincourts love playing cricket,' she said, 'and my poor darlings hate it, so they stop fielding almost at once and make daisy chains instead. As my brother's children don't mind as long as they can go on bowling and batting at each other everybody is happy . . . What magic did you use, Miss Whittingham, to persuade Mrs. Ravensbourne to provide Amy with such a pretty dress? Every time I have tried to send the child new clothes I have met with a blank refusal.'

'But I used no magic at all. Amy's dress is made from one of mine, and Mrs. Ravensbourne knows nothing about it.'

'Indeed?' Lady Ulsborne studied the muslin with a speculative eye. 'It is a very beautiful material. You must have looked very handsome in it, my dear.'

The charming warmth of the musical voice sent tears stinging suddenly behind Catherine's eyes and she turned her head away. 'I shall try to find some more dresses that may be pulled to pieces for Amy,' she said lightly. 'I have quite a number that I shall never wear again locked away in my trunk—' She broke off with a gasp of dismay. 'But I *didn't* lock it before I came out! ... I was in such haste to get Amy down the back stairs without being seen that I forgot.'

'Does it matter?' Lady Ulsborne glanced at her with smiling unconcern. 'Nothing will be stolen, surely?'

'I don't know.' Catherine spoke slowly, her face pale and distressed. 'I'm not worried about my own things ... anybody is welcome to them ... but it's Amy's little sandalwood box ...'

'A sandalwood box?' Lady Ulsborne, whose gloved fingers had been smoothing a crease in her dress, glanced at her companion curiously.

'Yes.' Catherine told her about the Chesters' visit and the present they brought Amy. 'I said I would take care of it for her, and this is how I have kept my promise! Suppose I find it gone when I get back?'

'But was there anything of value in it?'

'There were those bangles and the necklace she is wearing, and a small cotton bag of glass beads, and a letter and some official-looking documents. If Mrs. Ravensbourne had not told me that you were not to be here today I would have brought the box with me for you to see.'

'To whom was the letter addressed?'

'To Amy, with the request that she should read it on her twenty-first birthday.'

Again there came a curious glance from her companion, slightly sharper than before, while Lady Ulsborne's fingers continued to smooth the crease in her dress. 'Do you know who sent the box?' she asked.

'No. But there are some initials in silver on the lid ... M.S. entwined with J.B.T.'

'Oh no!' Helen Ulsborne gave a small gasp of dismay. 'How could anybody be so unwise as to send such a thing to poor little Amy? And in that house of all others!' She saw Catherine's look of bewilderment and recovered herself swiftly. 'It's a long story, Miss Whittingham, an unlucky business from start to finish, and all I can tell you about it is that my poor sister— Amy's mother—got herself entangled in a very sordid affair, and it looks as if the box and the letter may have been from her. But the poor girl is dead, and the thing is over and by way of being forgotten, and I think it would be very wise of you to bring me the box just as it is the next time you come here with Amy. I see no point in waiting until she is twenty-one and then stirring up mud that has settled with the years. It couldn't do any good to anybody, could it?'

'I should say that, on the contrary, it might do considerable harm. Amy is a sensitive little girl, and promises to be more so as she grows older.'

'Precisely. So I will tell you what we'll do. Bring me the box and the letter tomorrow morning—Miss Mattison can take Amy to play on the beach with the other children. I will give the letter to my husband to read, and if he says there is no harm in it, then I will keep it for her until she is twenty-one. But if he thinks there is anything in it that she should not see I will ask him to burn it, and simply keep the box and the documents for her.'

'It would certainly be less responsibility for me.' Catherine sounded relieved and Lady Ulsborne patted her arm and laughed.

'You take your duties too seriously, my dear! You should get on well with the Ravensbournes. They are so weighed down with the serious business of making money that they cannot think of anything else. I shall never forget William—Amy's father—when his old uncle died. I offered my condolences, naturally, though I could not endure the rude old man, and William said in his abrupt way: "Do you know, Helen, he only left one hundred thousand? What on earth did he do with the rest of the money he had out of the firm over all these years?" "Don't ask me," I said. "He didn't give it to me!" William was quite shocked, not because I spoke lightly of the dead, but because I joked about the sacred subject of "brass".'

It was at this moment that a man's voice said quietly behind them: 'Good afternoon, Helen. May a mere man ask the subject of such an earnest conversation on this lovely day? One would scarcely think Brighton gossip could be enough to cause such grave faces!' And William Ravensbourne was there beside them.

10

'We were talking about Amy,' said Lady Ulsborne quickly, while Catherine wondered how much he had overheard. 'She is growing very pretty, Will. I congratulate you on her looks!'

'Thank you.' His eyes left her animated face and went to his daughter, who had got the Ulsborne baby in her arms and was bringing him to Catherine, staggering under his weight.

'Look!' she cried as she came. 'He's cutting a second tooth! You can just see it coming through.'

Catherine ran to take the baby from her before he wriggled out of her arms.

'He is beautiful,' she agreed, smiling, 'but I'll take him back to his nurse for you, darling, while you go and say how d'you do to your father. He is here with Lady Ulsborne.'

'Oh, is he?' Amy looked without much concern at the man who had seated himself beside her aunt. 'Well, I'll say how d'you do if you think I must, but he won't mind if I don't.'

'But you must be polite, my love!'

Catherine went off with the baby while Amy walked reluctantly up to her father, and after greeting him solemnly waited for him to ignore her. But today he did not behave as usual: he took her outstretched hand and held it in his, drawing her towards him.

'That's a very pretty dress, Amy,' he said. 'Is it one of the new ones that Aunt Anna had made for you?'

'No,' said Amy with the bluntness that was so like his own, 'it isn't. It's made from one of Catherine's . . . Miss Whittingham's, I mean. And my shoes were given me by a friend of hers.'

The smile died out of her father's face and she blundered

on: 'There was only enough material for two schoolroom dresses, and it was an ugly dark grey, and the brown serge for my coat was the same colour that the Admiral Blake Orphanage children wear, and the boots that Great-Aunt Anna got me were so heavy and big that they made blisters on my feet.'

'Perhaps she thought you would grow into them!' said Lady Ulsborne, who had been listening with amusement, and she glanced at the man beside her with a touch of malice. 'I daresay she has forgotten how to buy clothes for children.'

Amy looked for Catherine, but having handed back the baby to his nurse she had remembered her neglected duty to Miss Mattison and had gone to sit beside her and help to umpire the game of cricket. Amy shifted from one foot to the other while her father remained silent, having apparently forgotten her, until, catching a smiling nod from her aunt, she ran off, greatly relieved. As he watched her go William Ravensbourne said slowly:

'I don't understand what is going on in Mecklinburgh Square. I told my aunt to get as many new dresses as the child needed . . . Damn it, Helen, I'm not a monster! And neither do I take kindly to accepting charity from Miss Whittingham and her friends.'

The sun had got round behind the trees and Lady Ulsborne shifted her lace parasol to keep it out of her eyes. 'I told you Amy was being neglected,' she reminded him, 'and you wouldn't believe me. You don't see enough of her, William, and your aunt's time is fully occupied with poor Edith.'

'Yes, that's it, of course.' He was anxious to agree with her. 'To be honest with you, Helen, I always thought you exaggerated my aunt's neglect of the child because you disliked her, but since having that letter from the Frenchwoman and making certain enquiries at Number Five, I don't think you were far wrong. I *haven't* seen enough of Amy, and I have been too ready to relinquish the care of her to others. If she has been neglected I have only myself to blame.'

'Well, I admit that I dislike your aunt. She frightens me to death! But I am equally aware that she has some excellent qualities that I lack—such as thrift, for example! Dick tells me that I don't know the meaning of the word.' Helen laughed and twirled the handle of her parasol. 'But I wouldn't take Mademoiselle's letter too seriously, all the same. The best governesses are full of fads and fancies, and you have to tread like a cat in case you offend their feelings, which are a great deal more sensitive than ours! Even my excellent Miss Mattison looks for snubs, and, what is more, she usually manages to find them!'

William Ravensbourne smiled abstractedly. 'Nevertheless when I took the matter up with my aunt I had an uncomfortable feeling that there was something wrong somewhere. There's a queer atmosphere in that house . . . I'd never noticed it before.'

'An atmosphere of . . . hate?' asked Lady Ulsborne softly, and now the handle of the parasol was still in her gloved hand.

'Perhaps.' He looked at her quickly. 'I'm not sure . . . But I intend to see much more of Amy, and I am going to remove her from Mecklinburgh Square as soon as I have found a home of her own for her to go to.'

'Your aunt won't like that.'

'On the contrary, I believe she may welcome the change, and I think Edith would be better for it, too. From what she let slip when I last saw her I feel that Amy's presence only serves to remind her of Mary, and her hatred for her is as strong as ever —' He broke off, remembering the warm, airless room, and Edith's pale face and glittering eyes as she had spoken of his wife. Hatred with some people was like love, in that it took a long time to die.

Lady Ulsborne put her hand on his arm. 'Our house is open to Amy whenever you say the word, William. You know that.'

'Yes, and I'm grateful to you and Richard for it. But I've shirked my responsibilities long enough. I want to make my daughter's acquaintance, and try to win her affection if I can.'

'Children are quick to forgive, and you are a young man still. One day you will marry again.'

'My aunt suggested that the other day.'

'And what did you say?'

He stooped to pick up the cricket ball that had rolled to their feet and threw it back to the players. 'I told her that the idea did not appeal to me.'

She did not pursue the subject. She did not believe that a man of his age and virility would have spent the last seven years without female consolation, and she had a very shrewd idea of where that consolation had been found, but it was not her business. She said she hoped they would see a great deal of Amy while they were in Brighton.

'Of course.' William's eyes rested for a moment on the

slender figure in grey that was seated beside the shorter stouter one of Miss Mattison. 'Miss Whittingham has my permission to bring Amy to see her cousins as often as you wish, as long as it does not interfere with her lessons.' When Catherine came up with Amy to say goodbye to Lady Ulsborne he repeated what he had said to his daughter's governess.

'That will be a delightful change.' Catherine looked pale and tired. 'Amy has no young friends in Brighton.' She would have taken her away then had he not stopped her.

'If you will wait a few minutes, Miss Whittingham, Lady Ulsborne's servant will get me a cab, and I will take you both back in it to Mecklinburgh Square.'

'Thank you, Mr. Ravensbourne, but I think it would be wiser for us to walk.'

'Why? Are you so anxious to take exercise? I should think that Amy has had enough racing about for one day.'

She smiled faintly, but she did not reply, and he appealed to his daughter. Already he was beginning to learn that if he wanted the truth he could be sure of getting it from her. 'Perhaps you will tell me, child. Wouldn't you like to come home with me in a cab?'

She shook her head. 'No,' she said decidedly. 'You see, a cab would drive up to the front door and we always go down the mews.'

'Down the mews? What on earth do you mean?'

'I think they have to use the servants' entrance, William,' said Lady Ulsborne lightly, and he flushed, and, seeing his annoyance, Catherine put in quietly:

'Mrs. Ravensbourne does not like noise because of disturbing Miss Edith, and so Amy and I go and come by the back stairs. It is the most sensible thing to do.' She held out her hand to her charge. 'Come along, dear. It is time we went.'

She took her off firmly, leaving William with a sense of frustration and a feeling of having been snubbed. He supposed he deserved it, after neglecting his daughter for so many years, but Miss Whittingham seemed uncommonly ready to put him in the wrong, and he did not like it. And yet there was a dignity about her and a pride in her dark eyes and pale face that convinced him that although he might not like her, she was the sort of young woman to whom he could safely trust Amy. She would impart to his daughter a sense of values and an integrity and honesty of purpose that had been unknown to the lovely, wayward creature who had stolen his senses and broken his heart . . .

In the meantime Catherine hurried home, scarcely listening to Amy's chatter about her cousins, her mind occupied once more by the thought of her unlocked trunk. There was no reason to suppose that anyone would visit the room in their absence because Mrs. Ravensbourne did not trouble herself about the nursery floor, and anything that went on there was simply reported to her by Pouncer. It was therefore ridiculous to have any apprehension about the trunk, and yet she knew she would not be happy until she got back to the room and found it as they had left it.

The doctor's brougham was outside Number Five as they passed by the top of the square: he often came to see Edith in the afternoon and could usually be persuaded to stay for a cup of tea. The mews, however, was silent and deserted as they came down into it along the little back lane. Cook was gossiping in the kitchen with Mrs. Stone, who always came to collect the laundry on Sunday evenings, ready for Monday's wash, and the back stairs were empty, the house beyond them silent as the grave.

They reached the third floor and Amy ran on to their bedroom and pushed open the door, and then stopped short with a little exclamation of surprise.

Catherine hurried after her, and stopped too, on the threshold, knowing that she had expected something of the sort.

Her trunk was standing open on the floor under the window, and the dresses that had been packed away in it were flung about the floor and over the beds, their lace trimmings torn and ribbons ripped off. Her mother's jewel-case was broken open, the jewellery thrown in a heap in the fireplace, although nothing was missing except a small cut-glass bottle of attar of roses that had been at the bottom of the case. At first glance it was as if a mischievous child had been at work, but there was more than mischief here.

Catherine cared nothing about the jewel-case, nor her dresses, nor the missing attar of roses.

There was only one thing that she wanted to find among the scattered contents of her trunk, and she knew before she began her feverish search that she would not find it.

The sandalwood box had gone.

*   *   *

It was a very worried Catherine who met Lady Ulsborne on the following morning.

'But did you make no enquiries, my dear?' asked Helen, after she had kissed Amy and sent her off to her cousins who were getting ready to go on the beach. 'I should have gone down to see Mrs. Ravensbourne if I'd been you, and insisted on her coming to look at the damage. It is a most disgraceful thing if you cannot leave the house for a few hours without having to lock up everything you possess.'

'I did think of speaking to Mrs. Ravensbourne,' said Catherine. 'But the doctor was there. I thought at first it was his usual Sunday visit to have tea with Edith, but Maggie told me later that Mrs. Ravensbourne had been out for a drive, leaving Edith asleep, and when she came back she found she had had a heart attack in her absence, and quite a sharp one, too. I couldn't worry her about the missing box just then.'

'Do you think Mrs. Ravensbourne could have taken it?'

'Oh dear me, no!' Catherine dismissed the thought. 'She wouldn't trouble with my things . . . I'm not so sure about Pouncer, but I don't think she would leave the room in such a state. She's the sly sort of woman who would be careful not to leave a trace of a search—if she happened to be looking for Amy's little box.'

'Who else knew about it? Albert? Maggie?'

'But they wouldn't take anything of Amy's. They're too fond of her to rob her of a sixpence. And, besides, it was Albert who smuggled it in to Amy in the first place. He might have lost his job over it.'

Lady Ulsborne looked perplexed. 'Was there any stranger there yesterday—anybody in the kitchen for instance?'

'Only the laundry-woman, Mrs. Stone, and she was enjoying her tea and gossip with Cook far too much to go rummaging about in the governess's room on the third floor!'

'Oh well, I wouldn't worry about it any more.' Helen dismissed the whole affair as an unsolved mystery. 'The sun is shining and the children are going on the beach. Let us send Amy with them while you and I take a drive along the front. I am heartily bored with my own company, and longing to have somebody to talk to—that is the worst of having a Member of Parliament for a husband. He is never with you when you want him. And the Selincourts are in Baden-Baden after their months in Paris. My brother says he has inherited Papa's gout, but I tell him his kind is brand-new and entirely his own. He drinks and eats far too much!'

So Amy drank a glass of milk and was despatched with her cousins to the beach, under the eye of Miss Mattison, while Catherine found herself being driven along the front towards Black Rock with Lady Ulsborne, and gradually the worry and anxiety left her in the luxury of being in a private carriage again, and listening to her companion's chatter. Nobody could be downcast for long with Helen Ulsborne: she was as gay as Bella, and much more sophisticated, with a ready wit and a charm that captivated poor Catherine and made her feel happier than she had been for a long time.

After that morning the days began to follow a pattern that was as enchanting as it was unexpected. At Number Five nothing was said about Amy's sandalwood box, and Mrs. Ravensbourne was far too concerned over Edith to care where the child went or with whom, and in fact she appeared to have washed her hands of her. But the meals in the schoolroom continued to be more plentiful, and every day Catherine found a fresh delight in the company of her new friend. Soon they were on the warmest terms, using each other's Christian names, and the weeks slipped by unnoticed. Bella's letters could be full of festivities now, but Catherine no longer envied her sister. What did it matter if she danced every night into the summer dawn? In the strange, lonely life that she had chosen for herself she had found a friend, and if the light-hearted companionship of Helen Ulsborne were to be only a fleeting one, at least she began to feel that life at Number Five was not entirely bad.

One rather stormy day as they were returning along the front they saw William Ravensbourne, but he did not see them.

'I did not know that Mr. Ravensbourne was still in Brighton,' said Catherine. 'I thought he had gone back to Yorkshire.'

Lady Ulsborne laughed. 'William doesn't always come to Brighton when he is in the South,' she said. 'He has a friend in Worthing with whom he stays. I have tried to get her name out of him but he won't tell me. He can be very close over things like that. All he will admit is that she is a widow from Yorkshire, and from that I feel I know exactly what she is like. I can picture her as being large and fair, you know, with plump feet thrust into high-heeled shoes several sizes too small for her, and a fondness for wearing quantities of unsuitable jewellery!'

Catherine did not answer. The sea that morning stretched out grey to the horizon, its rough surface broken by white horses, its yellow foam tumbling in over the grey shingle and then receding, leaving a mottled edge of grey and white. A sea no longer smiling but one that hid dark secrets in its grey depths. Beside her Lady Ulsborne rattled on:

'Poor William . . . I don't think he has any intention of marrying the lady, mind you, and I expect she knows it and is very accommodating in exchange for a pleasant house and a nice income!' She glanced at Catherine and laughed wickedly. 'Don't look so shocked! When you have known the Ravensbournes as long as I have few things will shock you any more!' And then she began talking about something else, but for the rest of the day the information that she had light-heartedly given remained stuck in Catherine's mind.

It was not her business what William Ravensbourne did, nor what friends he selected. She was only his daughter's governess. But this was a side to his character that General Whittingham's daughter found it hard to appreciate. A few days later, however, Mr. Ravensbourne's private concerns were overshadowed by something else.

'I can't wait to tell you the news I had from Dick this morning, Catherine,' said Lady Ulsborne, meeting her with a smiling face and waving the letter at her in triumph. 'He's got William's permission to have Amy with us in London to watch the Jubilee processions next week! We are taking our two eldest girls and Miss Mattison, leaving the younger ones with Nurse, and my only grief is that when the children and Miss Mattison come back to Brighton again I shall not be with them. I shall miss our drives and talks more than I can say, and I wish there was room in our plans for you, Catherine, but, alas, my love, there isn't! But you will be able to take a holiday and do what you please with your little self for the week while Amy is with us in London, so that will be a consolation!'

It did not occur to the charming little lady that Catherine could not take a holiday because she had nowhere to go. She certainly would not be welcomed in the house in Putney, where Miss Abbott was staying only on sufferance, and she could not afford to waste money on lodgings with a future as uncertain as hers. All she could do while Amy was away would be to stay on in Mrs. Ravensbourne's house, where she would scarcely be tolerated.

There was fortunately a great deal to do before the child could be ready in time to be called for by her aunt on her way to the station on Monday morning, and Amy was so excited that lessons became a farce. Her only fear was that her beloved Catherine would not be there when she came back, and Catherine had to promise a hundred times that nothing would shift her from Number Five in her absence.

'I shall be ready and waiting to hear all you have to tell me, my love, and you mustn't miss any of it up there in London, because I shall want to know it all.' She would not admit even to herself that she did not relish the prospect of being left alone in the empty floors at the top of the house.

It was only when she returned there after waving goodbye to the excited little girl on Monday morning that she felt her apprehensions closing in on her, as if in the very silence of the rooms there was a threat of danger and a hidden menace.

11

Breakfast had been cleared away in the garret schoolroom, and although the window and the skylight were open the air was already hot with the promise of another warm day. Certainly the old Queen seemed almost certain of a lovely week for her Jubilee, and as Catherine remembered that Bella would be there to watch and enjoy it all she was glad of it for her sake. Jubilees and jaunts to London were no longer for the elder Miss Whittingham.

She spent the morning dusting books, making a new timetable of lessons for when Amy returned, and in rearranging furniture and ornaments. Then, conscious of an aching head, she put on her hat and found her gloves and a parasol, and went for a walk along the front towards West Pier.

Not until July would the first of the day-trippers come thronging into the town: the pier was blessedly empty, and nobody spared her a glance as she walked alone up the echoing planks to the top and back again, missing the morning drive in Helen's carriage, and glad of the parasol that shielded her eyes from the glare of the sun on the sea.

She came to a seat from which she could see the panorama of the town spread out along the shore, the tall white houses and the large hotels, the parade and the rows of bathing machines on the beach below, and it seemed a lifetime ago since she and Bella had climbed up and down those slippery wooden steps. She had been sitting there a little while when a man stopped in front of her and took off his hat, and with some displeasure she recognized William Ravensbourne. She returned his greeting with a cool bow and was hunting for an excuse to get up and walk on when he forestalled her by sitting down beside her.

'Miss Whittingham,' he said, 'I was distressed to find that you had not been included in my sister-in-law's party when I went to see them off at Brighton station this morning. I thought you were to accompany Amy, and although I consider the enormous prices charged for seats on the procession route to be a great waste of money, I would have paid for one with pleasure rather than have you left behind like this. You must have thought such behaviour discourteous and unkind.'

'I did not think anything of the sort, Mr. Ravensbourne.' Catherine's voice was remote. 'I am employed here as Amy's governess: Miss Mattison has the two Ulsborne girls in her care and kindly said that one more for a week would make no difference. There was no need for anybody to consider me at all. I am quite content with my own company.'

He glanced at her curiously, as if he could not make her out. 'Do you prefer to be on your own, then?'

'Under some circumstances, yes.'

'Perhaps you are a young lady who likes to be discriminating in her choice of friends?' He prodded with his cane at the space between the planks of the pier, and as she did not reply, went on, 'In other words, Miss Whittingham, you consider that some people's company may be worse than none at all?'

'I did not say that.'

'No, but the implication was there.'

She wondered if he had taken it personally: she had no wish to provoke him, or indeed to arouse his interest in any way, but she had not met his type before. He looked more amused than annoyed, however, as he continued:

'That stiff manner of yours may be due to shyness: I don't remember having done anything to offend you—to the best of my knowledge I haven't exchanged more than a dozen words with you before today. But if you think that I have slighted you by any remark I have inadvertently made I can assure you that it was not meant. I've got to speak to you this morning, because I am in need of information.'

'Information?' The request was so unexpected that Catherine felt the ground cut away from under her feet, and the hint of a child that had been unnecessarily rude to its elders. 'About what, Mr. Ravensbourne?'

'About the things that have been going on in my aunt's house.'

She was further taken aback by what she took to be his effrontery.

'Do you mean to tell me that you don't know?' she cried, indignation getting the better of her.

'I would not ask you if I did,' he pointed out.

'But everything that has happened there must have been done under your orders, and with your full sanction!'

'I don't know what you mean.' There was no amusement now in his face: it was watchful and alert. 'I shall be glad if you will enlighten me.'

Catherine drew a deep breath. 'Amy is one of the dearest little girls in the world,' she said unsteadily, 'and it is no thanks to you, nor to your aunt, that she is not a little savage. The first time I saw her, her little face was smudged with dirt and tears, but she was dancing with a defiant courage in the empty attic that you dare to call her schoolroom. I had never seen a gentleman's child dressed in such rags before and I was horrified. There was no carpet on the floor, there were no curtains at the windows: a broken doll was her only toy, and there were a couple of books of moral tales, fifty years old. There was not a lesson-book in that so-called schoolroom, and Maggie reminded her that she was not allowed to dance because if your aunt caught her at it she would "whip her till the blood came" . . . Do you expect me to believe that you didn't know about these things? Did you never go upstairs to see Amy's schoolroom for yourself, and the wretched damp little bedroom with the plaster peeling from its walls—a room that a scullery-maid would not have tolerated? Do you honestly tell me, Mr. Ravensbourne, that you did not *know* that your daughter was being starved and ill-treated, that you did not *know* that her books were put on the fire, her dolls sent to church bazaars and any dresses Lady Ulsborne sent her given away because they were too good for her? You went to see her from time to time . . . these things *could* not happen without your knowledge and consent!'

He listened in silence while she poured out all her pent-up anger against him and his aunt, and it was only as she finished that she remembered that he had the power to dismiss her. She clasped her hands tightly over the handle of her parasol and said with more courage than she felt:

'I suppose you will give me notice for speaking like this, but I promised Amy I would be in Mecklinburgh Square when she returned, and I will keep that promise if I have to go to London and put the whole thing in front of our lawyer, Mr. Jason, of Lincoln's Inn Fields.' Her dark eyes met his stormily. 'When my father died Mr. Jason asked me to let him approach certain friends of his for help—friends who are not without importance in government and court circles. This assistance I refused for my sister and myself, but I would not hesitate to enlist it for little Amy, even if it meant exposing you and your heartless aunt.'

She stopped then, really frightened at what she had said, and stole a glance at him, but he was staring in front of him frowning, and as she finished he moved impatiently, pushed his hat to the back of his head, stretched out his legs and folded his arms.

'I have heard you out,' he said grimly. 'Now it is only fair that you should hear me. Your indictment is as unexpected as it is heavy, and I will say at once that it is not my habit to listen to threats, nor, fortunately for you, to answer them with others. As a Yorkshire friend of mine says, we will do no good by "calling each other". You have this much right on your side, however, that I *have* neglected my daughter, and for this I do deserve censure. I make no excuses for it: I never make excuses for my conduct to anybody. I am responsible for it to myself alone. My brothers tell me that I have one failing that will get me into serious trouble one day—that of trusting people too much. My reply has always been that I only trust them until they prove unworthy of my trust, and afterwards I never give them a farthing's worth of licence. But it would seem that in some cases this policy may be rather a more risky business than I had supposed, and in the meantime, Miss Whittingham, I would remind you that you are young and inexperienced in the ways of the world, and it would be as well for you not to judge people until you are aware of all the facts.' He unfolded his arms, shifted his hat to shield his eyes from the sun, and got up. 'Even I may not be quite so inhuman as you would like to believe! I am grateful to you, though, for having given me the information I wanted, which has only confirmed that already supplied by Mlle Birard.'

'Then . . .' She struggled to her feet, unable to leave things in so uncertain a state. 'I am to stay?'

'Of course you are to stay.' He studied her embarrassed face with a somewhat grim smile. 'Have you received a salary since you have been in Mecklinburgh Square?'

'No . . . that is to say, Lady Ulsborne was going to arrange something with you about it.'

'And in her usual feather-brained way Lady Ulsborne has forgotten all about it. Did she state the amount you were to receive from me?'

Catherine remembered Mrs. Trantam's advice about her attitude towards money. 'I believe twenty-five pounds a year was mentioned,' she said reluctantly.

'As little as that? You'd much better work in my mills, my lass! You'd make more money! But let's get it settled.' He produced a wallet from his breast pocket and selected five crisp white five-pound notes from it. 'Here is a year's salary, and here is my hand on a contract between us, Miss Whittingham. Break it at your peril!' But there was a twinkle at the back of his eyes as he put the notes into her left hand and held out his right to take hers in a firm grip. 'I hope you will enjoy your week's holiday in Brighton!' And with that he released her hand and left her.

Catherine walked back to her solitary lunch in the schoolroom in a thoughtful mood.

It seemed she had made a mistake in fixing the blame for Amy's treatment on her father, and yet if Mrs. Ravensbourne were not acting under her nephew's orders, to whom was she responsible for her persistent ill-treatment of the child? Because there was no doubt at all that somebody was behind the old Yorkshirewoman in the matter, somebody who would gain satisfaction from knowing that Amy was half starved and frightened, somebody who had chosen that attic for her schoolroom and the miserable bedroom with its damp, stained walls. But, she could no longer believe that Amy's father was that somebody, because although he had not said a great deal, she was convinced that he had been secretly as angry as she was about it all.

The morning's meeting on the pier nagged at her through

the long afternoon. She felt she had to know more about her employer and his family, and in the evening she made her way to Mrs. Westcott's neat little house.

The dressmaker was at home and welcomed her kindly, asking if she had found some more dresses that she could alter for Amy.

'I have some white linen tennis skirts and blouses which could be made into pleated skirts and sailor blouses for her, but I did not come to see you about that because she is away for a week with her aunt, Lady Ulsborne, in London. Sir Richard has taken seats for them all to watch the Jubilee processions.'

'How kind of him! But then Sir Richard Ulsborne is a very kind gentleman, far too generous and open-handed for his means, I've heard, and I'm afraid Lady Ulsborne will not help him to save his money. But I ought not to talk to you like this, Miss Whittingham. It is none of my business.'

'But that is why I have come to you,' said Catherine with a worried little frown. 'I'd like to know more about Amy's mother, Mrs. William Ravensbourne, and all I have been able to discover is that she was involved in a scandal some years ago, and nobody wants to talk about it.'

Mrs. Westcott looked thoughtful. 'What I could tell you would only be gossip,' she said, 'because I never came into contact with such people. But there is one person who knows all about it, and that is old Mrs. Thatcher, who lives at Number Eight. She used to be nurse in the Selincourt family years ago, and brought up Lady Ulsborne and her sister from babyhood. You can't miss the house—she has a large tabby cat she sets great store on, and he's always sitting sunning himself in the bay window.'

Catherine thanked her and walked on down the terrace until she came to Number Eight, and there, sure enough, was the tabby cat, with his paws folded under him on the window-sill, and a little old lady with snow-white hair knotted back in a bun, and a smiling rosy face, seated on a Windsor chair out on the step.

Directly she knew who she was, Mrs. Thatcher was delighted to see her, and invited her in to have a cup of tea.

'I was just going to make myself some,' she said. 'It will be no trouble to fetch an extra cup, and there's a home-made cake my daughter brought me yesterday.' She showed her with pride into the front room, where some flourishing geraniums shared the window with the cat, and bustled off to get out her best cups and saucers. Left to herself, Catherine examined the photographs that adorned the chimney-piece, the one in the centre being of a large mansion with a carriage drawn up at the door, and on either side of it portraits of two young women, one whom she recognized at once as Lady Ulsborne, and the other so like her that it could be no other than Amy's mother. But Mary was far more beautiful, and there was a grave enchantment in her smile and the turn of her fair head that made Catherine want to smile back at her.

Mrs. Thatcher came back with her tray and put it down on the table in the middle of the room before joining Catherine at the empty fireplace.

'You are looking at Miss Mary, I see,' she said. 'That's Miss Amy's mother. She was the Hon. Mary Selincourt when that portrait was taken. And that's Selincourt Castle where they lived with their father, Lord Selincourt, and that's their brother, the present Lord Selincourt, sitting in the carriage. He sold the castle when he came into the title. I think a London business man bought it.'

'What was Miss Mary like?' asked Catherine.

'Miss Mary?' The old woman smiled and there was a tender light in her eyes. 'She was the loveliest creature I ever set eyes on in my life, nor ever will see again. You couldn't help loving her while you scolded, and I was always scolding her, because she was the wildest and most wicked girl I'd ever had to nurse. "Miss Mary," I said to her time and again, "you'll come to a bad end, see if you don't. That isn't the way young ladies should behave." But she didn't care. She would give me a hug that took the breath from my body, and off she would go, flying about the hills on her little mare, outstripping Mr. Terence and the grooms, plaguing the life out of her father with wanting this and that, and his lordship without a penny piece. "I shall marry the richest man who asks me," she used to say, "because money is the only thing that matters." "Now, Miss Mary," I'd say, "you've no call to talk like that. You know it's love that matters in marrying." And in the end, of course, it was love that was her undoing ... But there, it's all over and done with now, and she's dead, poor lamb. Mr. Ravensbourne came to tell me of her death when he was in Brighton recently.'

'Did Miss Mary know Mr. Ravensbourne for long before she married him?'

'Bless you, yes, miss! Mr. Terence brought him to stay one

summer during the long vacation. He was a nice young man, blunt-spoken, but with an open way with him that made you like him, and there was no doubt about his money. He fell in love with Miss Mary the moment he met her, and he never looked at another afterwards. She wouldn't have him at first: there were plenty of young men after her, young Captain Tempest among them.'

'Captain Tempest?' Catherine sounded startled.

Mrs. Thatcher looked at her quickly. 'Yes ... have you met him, miss?'

'No ... but I've heard of him.'

'And you are not the only one!' remarked Mrs. Thatcher drily. She poured out a cup of tea for Catherine, pressing upon her a large slice of seed cake, and went on:

'I went up to stay with Mrs. William Ravensbourne when Miss Amy was on the way. Mr. Ravensbourne wrote to me himself and asked me if I would go and keep his wife company, as she was lonely and bored. I don't know what sort of place I expected to find up there in Yorkshire: it was a great, new, red-brick barracks of a house, with gardens all laid out beautiful, and great heavy curtains at the windows, and Turkey carpets everywhere, and even a bathroom for the servants. At the castle there was no bathroom at all and our wages were always in arrears, and I often wondered why we stayed. But stay we did, and every night his lordship and his family would sit down to dinner waited on by the butler and three footmen, the silver and cut-glass sparkling under the chandeliers, and the young ladies dressed as if royalty was coming, though their dresses were only made by the village dressmaker. Up in Yorkshire Mrs. Ravensbourne spent a fortune on Miss Edith's clothes, which were all made in London, and they said it cost a thousand a year to dress her. But after Miss Amy was born, when Miss Helen came to stay with her sister and they went to balls together, it was my two young ladies that the men fought to dance with, and poor Miss Edith was a wallflower, often as not. Miss Helen and Miss Mary laughed about her a great deal, just as they laughed at her mother and at Mr. William, who was head of Ravensbourne's by then. But I've never seen a man so ready to give his wife everything she wanted. Jewels, dresses, sables, carriages, horses to ride—whatever she wanted, she had only to mention it and the thing was done. He worshipped her and she took full advantage of it, and so did Miss Helen. He was good to his lordship, too, lending him money to put the castle in order and never asking for it back. Miss Helen laughed about that too. "Poor Will," she said to me, "he'll never see his money again!" Miss Helen was like her sister, only not so lovely and lacking her wildness and self-will. But both had the trick of saying things about people that would make you laugh at the time, and only afterwards it came to you that they were cruel as well. Some people may be natural figures of fun, but they shouldn't be ridiculed because they don't know what to talk about at a dinner-table, nor how to dress, and because they haven't got portraits of famous ancestors hanging on their walls.'

'So they laughed at Mr. Ravensbourne?'

'Why yes, but mostly to his face, which was better than going behind his back, and he had a quiet way with him that shamed them sometimes.'

Catherine's thoughts went back wryly to her conversation with him that morning: certainly he could make one feel ashamed without saying a great deal.

'He's a good man, is Mr. Ravensbourne,' continued old Mrs. Thatcher. 'A fine man—far finer than that Captain Tempest.'

Catherine asked quietly, 'What happened?'

Mrs. Thatcher sighed and smoothed the apron that was tied over her neat cotton dress. Then she poured out another cup of strong sweet tea for her visitor and insisted on her taking another slice of seed cake before she went on:

'Everything went smoothly until Captain Tempest came to stay. I'm afraid he and Miss Mary thought it all out before he came: they knew that Miss Edith was to have a substantial sum of money when she married, and the Captain hadn't a penny. There were balls in plenty that summer in Yorkshire— Miss Amy was just a year old—and there were moonlight picnics and boating parties on the lake and so on, and it wasn't long before Miss Edith and Captain Tempest were engaged to be married.'

'But . . . I thought Captain Tempest was in love with Miss Mary? . . . Mrs. Ravensbourne, I mean.'

The old woman gave her a glance that was half amused, half pitying and wholly wise.

'I don't say he was ever in love with Miss Edith. I'm only saying that he got himself engaged to her. He was very handsome, was Captain Tempest, and very charming, and no woman he set out to win could ever resist him. I don't suppose Miss Edith had ever met anyone like him before, and he fair dazzled her, and after their engagement was announced she looked so radiant that there wasn't one of us that didn't hope it would work out well for her, poor young lady.' Mrs. Thatcher put her empty cup down on the tray.

'I have sometimes wondered if Miss Mary and the Captain didn't start it all just to tease Miss Edith and Mr. Ravensbourne. Miss Mary detested Miss Edith and was always trying to make her husband jealous. But once the Captain was engaged things seemed to get out of hand. He and Miss Mary were like a pair of mischievous children that had set fire to a field of stubble and couldn't put it out, try as they would. I remember the night they ran away together as clearly as if it was yesterday. Miss Mary came to find me that evening in the nursery where I was putting the finishing stitches into one of Miss Amy's dresses, and she hugged me and said: "I've been a naughty girl to you, but you still love me, don't you? You'll love me whatever I do?" I felt something was wrong and I said more roughly than I should, "What have you been up to this time?" But she only gave a queer little laugh and told me that I'd understand in the morning. And the next day I heard that she had gone off with Captain Tempest.'

'Did Mr. Ravensbourne . . . divorce her?'

'No. At first he was too stunned to think of it, and then he hoped that she would tire of the Captain and come back to him. But when I offered to go on looking after Miss Amy he told me that he did not think my upbringing had been very successful and he'd rather have his daughter raised to his own standard . . . You could understand him being bitter and angry, poor man, and nobody blamed him for it, least of all me.'

'How did Miss Edith take it?'

'She was terribly ill for a long time. She started those dreadful heart attacks about then, and I believe she's had them ever since. Her mother brought her down here to Brighton and Miss Amy came with them, but I didn't see them again until my married daughter moved down here and Mr. Ravensbourne bought this cottage for me to be near her. He knew that I'd loved Miss Mary, bad as she was, and he always thought that if her mother had lived she wouldn't have turned out so wild. It's a sad thing for young people to grow up without a mother.'

'And with no Aunt Em either,' thought Catherine, with an affectionate memory of the aunt who had taken their mother's place as long as she could remember.

But it was getting late, and tomorrow would be Jubilee Day.

She thanked the old lady for her help, admired the geraniums and the cat, told her about Amy's visit to London with Lady Ulsborne and walked back slowly to Mecklinburgh Square.

12

For the rest of the evening Catherine was haunted by the story she had heard, and she thought she began to understand the secret of the sandalwood box. If Mary Ravensbourne had been the woman her old nurse had described such a gift to her daughter would have been typical of the cruel gaiety of her nature. The present was planned to shock Mrs. Ravensbourne and her nephew, and to puzzle Amy, forcing them to tell her the scandalous truth about her mother. Under such circumstances it was an excellent thing that the box had disappeared and she hoped that whoever had taken it had put it on the kitchen fire.

The next morning, that of the Jubilee celebrations, dawned mistily at first with the promise of a hot day. The air was still, the sea calm, and the day having been declared a general holiday even Albert had been told that he could take the day off. He was already dressed in his Sunday suit with an enormous red, white and blue favour in his buttonhole when he brought Catherine's breakfast up to her, and as he deposited the tray on the table in the deserted schoolroom he told her he was going to join his friends in watching the gathering of the Volunteers for the big parade in Preston Park.

'All the First Sussex Volunteer Artillery is to be there, miss,' he said. 'Colonel Noble, he's commanding it. And there's a battalion of the Royal Sussex Regiment under Colonel Verrall, and there's the Infantry Brigade, and the massed bands, and the Artillery's bringing guns to fire the salute. You ought to come to the park too, miss, and watch it all. You'll never see the like of it again most likely, not in all your life.'

Catherine smiled at his excited face and said she would do her best to be there, and he went off, whistling 'Rule Britannia' more loudly than he would dare on any ordinary day. After she had finished her breakfast, alone in the top of the house, Catherine felt restless and unable to occupy her mind or her fingers: sewing was tedious and reading impossible with the thought of all the excitement and bustle going on in the town.

She changed her black dress for a grey cotton and put on a white sailor hat with a black ribbon, and went out into the flag-lined streets, where, from ten o'clock onwards, crowds had been gathering. The pier had flags fluttering down its entire length, and banners strung from lamp to lamp, but the regatta was not timed until the afternoon, and she turned her face towards the town.

Here every shop window was festooned with bunting, and every shop front had the royal cipher or the coat of arms in gold on purple, loyal inscriptions being picked out in gold and coloured lights, ready for the illuminations later on. As Catherine paused in front of one of the biggest shops in the town the windows above were opened and the young ladies employed there sang the National Anthem: the crowds on their way to the park gathered to listen and to applaud and to join in, the young men taking off their straw boaters, the girls in their light summer dresses flushed and smiling as if they had been curtseying to the Queen.

Catherine walked on and at the General Post Office the same thing happened, the telegraph staff singing the anthem, while in the park the sixteen-pounders began booming out their salute of twenty-one guns, and the massed bands struck up 'Soldiers of the Queen'. It was as if all over the town, just as it was happening all over the country, people had suddenly realized that this was one of the greatest days in the life of the old lady at Windsor, and that for sixty years she had ruled over them and done that difficult and thankless task remarkably well.

Catherine wished she had little Amy with her. She missed the little hand in hers, the light feet that danced along the pavements beside hers. Brighton schools were to keep Thursday that week as the children's day, but the church that she and Amy attended, St. David's, was just inside the Hove boundary, and on the previous Sunday, at the end of the Thanksgiving Service, Catherine had offered her assistance at the school sports that were planned for that afternoon. Her offer had been gratefully accepted by the Vicar and his wife, Mrs. Cranston, and feeling now that it was more than likely that the governess's lunch in Mecklinburgh Square would have been forgotten in the excitement of the day, Catherine took herself into a teashop and lunched frugally off a cup of tea and a sandwich, and walked on to St. David's Vicarage.

The neat house-parlourmaid who answered the door told her that the Vicar and his wife were down at the schoolhouse marshalling the children before their teachers took them off to join the others from the Hove schools in New Church Road. Catherine went on to the schoolhouse, to be greeted with delight by Mrs. Cranston, an energetic lady who had long ago become the unpaid curate in her husband's parish.

'We'll see the children off,' she said, 'and then you can come to the Recreation Ground with me and help count the Jubilee mugs. There should be three hundred for our children, and every child is to have cake and a bag of sweets and a drink of lemonade before the sports start.' She broke off. 'Fancy the dear old Queen reaching her Diamond Jubilee! I was thinking this morning as I dressed that I don't remember a time in England when Queen Victoria was not on the throne. She has been reigning all my life, and I've a grown-up daughter! ... I do hope the excitement today won't be too much for the dear old lady. If anything happened to her one feels it would be the end of the world!'

The Vicar was near enough to raise his eyebrows over this remark. 'My dear!' he expostulated. 'The end of an epoch perhaps, but not the end of the world! The Prince of Wales would come into his own then, poor man! He has waited long enough.'

'It would feel most peculiar to have a king, all the same,' said Mrs. Cranston decidedly. 'I don't think I'd like it very much!' She picked up a purple banner with the words 'God Bless Victoria' on it in silver and thrust it into his hands. 'Somebody has forgotten his banner! I should say it is Dennis Barker, in the second rank from the front. See if you can find him, dear, and tell him he is not to let go of it again.'

The children were forming up quickly in the road outside the church school, the little girls with clean, starched pinafores over their frocks, hats and sun-bonnets on their heads to protect them against the sun, the boys in their Sunday-best suits and caps, their boots laced up neatly, their black woollen stockings pulled up above the knee. They all looked very hot, very excited, very happy, and were only waiting the Vicar's words to march away behind him to New Church Road. When the last of them was out of sight Catherine and Mrs. Cranston hurried off to the Recreation Ground, and had got the mugs and refreshments set out on the trestle tables there before the head of the procession entered the drive at three.

For the next hour or so small boys ran races and jumped and little girls skipped and drilled and sang patriotic songs, and everybody got hot and sticky and one or two mugs were broken, while Catherine was taken into a tent to judge an exhibition of needlework which had in some curious way been included in the day's events, but as every piece of work there had some suitable motif worked into it one could not say that it was not right for the occasion.

While she pondered over the merits of a purple pincushion with 'Victoria, 1837–1897' worked on it in silver, a tablecloth embroidered in thistles, roses, shamrocks, and leeks, and a cushion cover exhibiting Windsor Castle in red and blue cross-stitch on a white ground, the sports had finished, the prizes been given, and the children were going. Catherine suddenly found herself choosing Windsor Castle and being warmly thanked and dismissed, her task ended, with an empty evening in front of her and the town still in a holiday mood.

The regatta was over, but the pier was still thronged with people waiting for the bonfires to be lighted on the distant beacons and the fireworks that were to start directly it was dark. The sea was out, the waves running in lazily, as waves often seem to do in the late afternoon of a summer's day: gone was the busy sparkle of the morning, the dancing shimmer of sunshine on blue water, but Catherine was in no hurry to reach the garret schoolroom and the solitary hours that awaited her there.

She had become accustomed to walking alone, but as she strolled along she knew that it would be impossible for her to go out after dark by herself. A great number of Volunteers had been loyally drinking their old Sovereign's health until they were very tipsy indeed, and already she had to step off the pavement once or twice to avoid a string of staggering uniforms that stretched across it.

She left the sea-front reluctantly and was turning up a narrow street that would take her to the near side of Mecklinburgh Square on her way home when three Volunteers reeled out of a public house across her path, arm-in-arm and singing at the tops of their voices. At the same moment she was seen a view halloo was uttered, and she threw dignity to the winds and picked up her skirts and ran.

Fortunately they were too drunk to follow her far and contented themselves with shouting and whistling after her, but she was too frightened to stop, and went on running down the street until she was brought up sharply by a man coming unexpectedly round the corner.

'It isn't wise to be out alone on a day like this, Miss Whittingham,' said William Ravensbourne quietly, taking her arm to steady her. 'May I take you back to my aunt's house?'

'Thank you. I'd be glad of your company.' Catherine found to her disgust that she was trembling, and she glanced back over her shoulder at the noisy Volunteers. 'It was my fault, not theirs! . . . I've grown so accustomed to going about alone with Amy, as her protector, that it never occurred to me that I could be in need of one myself! Those days are past for me.'

'That's rather a sad thing for anyone as young as you to be saying—or even thinking,' he said gently. 'Where is your sister today?'

'In London with the Trantams.'

'Is Mrs. Trantam there as well?'

'Oh yes. Her house has been shut up for some time.'

'You must think me a very unobservant sort of chap, but I never noticed it. But with Amy away I daresay my aunt is glad of your company at meals, and in the drawing-room after Edith is in bed?'

She smiled faintly. 'Mrs. Ravensbourne prefers to have her meals alone with her daughter, and they like to have the drawing-room to themselves.'

'But . . .' He looked so concerned that she felt bound to reassure him.

'Mr. Ravensbourne, please don't worry about me. I have plenty to occupy my time until Amy comes back, and there is a nice view from my attic room. I can watch the crowds and the fireworks from there tonight and amuse myself very well.' He did not reply and she stumbled on unhappily: 'I am glad I met you this evening, because I wanted to apologize for the things I said to you yesterday morning. I always flattered myself that I did not jump to conclusions about people I did not know, but I seem to have done so unwarrantably this time. I ought to have waited until I had learned more about you.'

'Learned more about me?' He frowned and asked curtly: 'From whom?'

Too late she regretted her impulsively spoken words. He had every right to be angry with her for what must seem to be unpardonable prying into his private affairs, and she said more unhappily still that she had been talking to Mrs. Thatcher.

'Nancy Thatcher!' He made a wry grimace. 'One of the biggest gossips that ever lived. But she was devoted to my wife.'

'She was not blind to her faults, though,' said Catherine timidly, and repented her rashness again when his frown returned abruptly.

'My wife had no faults,' he said with a curtness that silenced her. 'They were all on my side.'

She dare not say any more and they walked on without speaking until they arrived in Mecklinburgh Square, when he left her on the doorstep of Number Five with an abrupt good night. The door was opened by a breathless Maggie, ready dressed to go out.

'Oh, I'm so glad you've come back, miss!' she said. 'Pouncer said I wasn't to leave Miss Edith, and she'd only be out for a minute, but she's been gone nearly an hour. My young man was meeting me at the pier at seven, and it's gone half-past now.'

'But isn't Mrs. Ravensbourne in?'

'No, miss. That friend of hers, Mrs. Wainwright from the other side of the square, come in her carriage and asked if the mistress and Miss Edith wouldn't like to drive round with her and see the decorated streets and the lights in the Pavilion Gardens, but Miss Edith had a headache and wouldn't go, so the mistress told Pouncer to stay with Miss Edith while she went. Well, I've got the evening off and so has Cook, and I was just coming down into the kitchen putting on my gloves when Pouncer comes along with her hat on. "Maggie," she says, "Miss Edith is asleep and I'm going as far as the pillar-box for a breath of air. I can see the decorations tomorrow," she says. "They won't take all them down overnight. I'll be back in a few minutes." And that was at half-past six!'

'Well, you may go now,' said Catherine, smiling. 'I shall be in the schoolroom all the evening and I'll leave the baize door open at the foot of the attic stairs so that I can hear if Miss Edith rings her bell. Run along, or that young man of yours will be off with some other girl!'

'Thank you, miss.' Maggie beamed her gratitude. 'I've put your supper in the schoolroom. It's only bread and cheese and a glass of milk, but Cook didn't leave anything else for you.'

'It will do very well, thank you.'

'Thank you, miss. Good night.'

'Good night, Maggie.'

Catherine went up the stairs quietly. There was not a sound from Edith's room and the nearer she got to the roof the warmer the house became, until the heat on the top floor was stifling, and she was glad to hook back the baize door to let the air come through.

She had just finished her supper when she thought she heard a slight noise, and for the first time it occurred to her that except for the invalid two floors below she was alone in the big house. She got up and went to the top of the attic stairs and listened, and again she thought she heard a slight movement in the house, followed by a faint sound like a door being opened or closed.

'It's Pouncer back again,' she told herself. 'No need to be nervous!'

She went down the stairs rather reluctantly, however, and waited on the landing below for a few minutes, conscious of her own beating heart. The house was so silent that it seemed to be waiting and listening too, and annoyed with herself for having given way to nerves she went on down to the empty kitchens. But the back door was locked and bolted, the shutters were up at the windows, and the area door was still locked from the outside, with the key under the scraper so that the servants could get in that way. It seemed evident that Pouncer was not yet back.

She returned more slowly up the back stairs to the third floor again, and as she came out on to the corridor she saw that her bedroom door was open.

She was certain that she had left it shut, and she went into the room quickly and looked round, but at first glance everything was as she had left it: her hat was on the bed, her gloves beside it with her parasol. Then she noticed a ribbon hanging from a half-opened drawer as if somebody had been searching for something there and left in a hurry.

Nothing appeared to have been taken, however, and she put it tidy again and shut it, puzzled and resentful at having her belongings gone through in this fashion. She closed the bedroom door firmly behind her and was about to return to the schoolroom upstairs when she heard a scream, followed by a muffled thud from the direction of the main staircase.

She ran along the corridor and was half-way down the stairs before she was stopped by what she took at first glance to be a bundle of clothes lying at the bottom, and was horrified to find Edith Ravensbourne there, lying unconscious on the corridor below.

13

It was then that Catherine realized fully how alone she was: there was not even Albert or Maggie who could be sent for help. She turned Edith over gently and found to her relief that she was still breathing, although in the dying light over the stairs she looked deathly white.

'Brandy,' thought Catherine desperately. 'I wonder where Mrs. Ravensbourne keeps it?' But knowing the thrifty mistress of the house she guessed that she had taken the keys of the cupboards with her when she went out. There was, however, a small flask of her own in her trunk, one that she had taken with her when she went abroad with Bella and Miss Abbott in the past. She had not unpacked it since she came to Mecklinburgh Square and she ran now and fetched it, and lifting Edith in her arm she forced a little between her lips.

The girl stirred, groaned and then opened her eyes.

'What happened?' she asked, and then, more faintly: 'I was looking for somebody to come and help me and I tripped and fell . . .'

'You will be all right now.' Catherine tried to reassure her. 'Take another sip of this and then lay still.' She held the flask to the white lips a second time and was relieved to see a little colour return to them. 'Can you move?' she asked. 'Do you think you have broken any bones?'

'I don't know.' Edith closed her eyes again. 'Fetch my mother.'

'I will directly she comes in. But in the meantime I would like to get you downstairs and into bed. I'll go and see if any of the servants are back yet.'

'Don't leave me . . . I might die!' The thin hands that clutched at hers were stronger than they looked. 'You can't leave me here alone in the dark . . . I won't let you!'

'Very well. I will stay.' Catherine made her as comfortable as she could and sat down beside her on the stairs while the light faded from the window and the staircase grew shadowed and dark, and it was not until half-past eight that the welcome sound of the front-door bell jangled far away in the basement.

Edith seemed to have fallen asleep and Catherine released herself gently and ran down the three flights of stairs to the front door and found Mr. Ravensbourne on the doorstep.

'Oh!' she said without giving him time to speak. 'I'm so glad you have come back . . . I'm alone here and Edith has had a bad fall. I'm afraid she is very ill.'

'Where is she?' He dropped his hat and stick in the hall and raced up the stairs in front of her two at a time.

'At the bottom of the staircase leading up to the nursery floor.' Catherine followed him as fast as she could.

'The nursery floor? What in the world was she doing there?'

'I don't know.' There would be time later to find the answers to such questions: all that mattered now was to have his help. She lit the gas in the corridor where Edith lay and when he saw his cousin, William gave a dismayed whistle of concern.

'Is she asleep?' she whispered as he knelt down beside her.

'No . . . I rather think she's unconscious.' He thought a moment. 'I'll carry her down to her room. She isn't very heavy, and I've carried her before. Then I'll have to leave her with you while I go for a doctor. I suppose my aunt is out?'

'She went with Mrs. Wainwright to watch the fireworks.'

'And the servants are out too?'

'Yes, though I can't understand why Pouncer isn't back. She told Maggie she was only going out for a few minutes, and that was long before seven.'

'And it's now close on nine. Oh well, I suppose even Pouncer is human sometimes.' With Catherine's help he lifted his cousin up in his arms and took her down to her bedroom on the first floor. He was immensely strong. She did not regain consciousness as he laid her down on the bed, and Catherine covered her warmly and began to rub her wrists.

'Go as quickly as you can,' she said. 'I'll stay here with her until you bring the doctor back with you.'

He did not ask if she was afraid of being left: he knew that she was as equal to meet emergencies as he was, and he went away, but as he came out on the steps Mrs. Wainwright's carriage turned into the square. He waited to tell his aunt what had happened before going off for the doctor, and Mrs. Ravensbourne hurried into the house and up to Edith's room, where she pushed Catherine unceremoniously away and bent over the bed, her florid face convulsed and agonized.

'Edith!' she cried. 'What happened, love?' She turned fiercely on Catherine. 'Where is Pouncer? Why did she allow this to happen? I told her Edith was not to be left for a moment.'

In a low voice Catherine told her all she knew.

'She regained consciousness for a few minutes after I found her,' she added. 'I gave her some brandy then, but I haven't dared to give her any since in case I choked her. Have you any smelling salts?'

'On the table on the far side of the bed.' Mrs. Ravensbourne glanced at the cut-glass brandy flask with its silver cup. 'That's not mine!'

'No, it's the one I used to take on journeys: my sister wasn't a good traveller.'

'Where did you say you found Edith?'

'At the bottom of the stairs to the nursery floor.'

Mrs. Ravensbourne did not seem to share her nephew's surprise: she sighed and said she would be glad when the doctor came. 'Though I doubt if Will finds him at home on a night like this. Everybody's going mad over these stupid fireworks.'

Through the open window Catherine could hear the occasional crack of a rocket and the somewhat derisive cheering of the crowds that watched them: they were let off at too-infrequent intervals for the temper of those who celebrated Jubilee night. She thought: 'Sixty years . . . I suppose Edith was born when the Queen had been reigning thirty years . . . and she may die tonight.' She said in a low voice: 'Her hands are very cold. Shall I fetch some hot water from the bathroom?'

'There are hot bricks in the little oven beside the range in the kitchen,' said Mrs. Ravensbourne. 'You will find flannel cases for them on a towel-rack near by. Run and get a couple and we'll put them at her feet. Pouncer would have done all that if she had been here. I can't think why she is staying out like this. She has never done it in all the twenty years she has been with me, and she'll have a piece of my mind when she comes in!'

Catherine sped away and was soon back with the hot bricks, and they had no sooner got them to the invalid's feet when William Ravensbourne came back with the doctor.

'I was lucky to catch Dr. Byrne,' William said as Catherine opened the door to them. 'He was only just in from an accident.'

'It's been a day of accidents,' grumbled the doctor. 'No celebrations for me today. All I've been doing is treating the casualties—faints from the heat, heart attacks, and broken limbs among children who climbed trees to get a better view!'

Catherine took him upstairs and William was about to follow them when a man stepped out from the shadows at the foot of the steps and called to him softly. 'Name of Ravensbourne, sir?' he asked.

'Yes.' As the light from the doorway fell on him William saw the uniform of a police constable. 'Do you want anything?'

'Well, sir, I saw the doctor's carriage here and I don't want to add to trouble if there's illness in the house, but perhaps you can tell me if a person by the name of Pouncer lives here?'

'She is my aunt's maid.' He saw the man's grave face. 'Has anything happened to her?'

'I'm sorry, sir, but I'm afraid it has . . . She was knocked down as she was hurrying across the road from the pillar-box this evening—the cabby said he couldn't avoid her. She just walked into his hoss without looking, as you might say . . . and in short, sir, the poor woman is dead.'

* * *

That night, when all the world outside seemed to be enjoying itself, seemed endless to Catherine, as she took turns with Mrs. Ravensbourne in watching by Edith's bed.

At ten o'clock the servants returned and she went down at their mistress's request to tell them what had happened, and while they went upstairs quietly to bed, in the square outside Edith's windows the red, white and blue fairy-lights flickered in the trees, and from the parade chanting voices and bursts of laughter reminded those who cared to listen that it was still a carnival night.

Not until dawn did Edith recover consciousness and when her cousin called to enquire after her later on that morning it was a heavy-eyed Miss Whittingham who went down to the dreary little morning-room to give him what news she could.

'I was so thankful that you had come back,' she said, 'that I never thought to ask you what you had come for—I hope it was not important?'

He glanced at her pale face thoughtfully. 'No,' he said quietly. 'It was not important.' It was scarcely the time to tell her that, stirred with compunction and a feeling of pity for her, he had returned quixotically to offer his company and protection on a sight-seeing tour of the town. 'Miss Whittingham,' he went on abruptly, 'I know my aunt. Now that Pouncer has gone she will never consent to engage a stranger to help her nurse Edith, and she will only share that burden with somebody she trusts. I know that she trusts you. In short, if I telegraph to the Ulsbornes to keep Amy with them for a few weeks will you be willing to help Aunt Anna with poor Edith?'

She did not let him see how dismayed she was at the thought of it: she was quite sure that Edith would dislike the arrangement, and she did not share his opinion that his aunt trusted her. 'If Mrs. Ravensbourne wishes it I will, of course, do all I can,' she said unwillingly.

'Thank you.' He looked relieved, and after she had gone upstairs again to Edith he joined his aunt in the breakfast-room where she was trying to swallow some toast and marmalade and a cup of tea and put the same proposition to her. She agreed with surprising mildness that it would be the best solution.

'Unless Edith objects,' she added.

'Doesn't she like Miss Whittingham, then?'

She shrugged her shoulders. 'You know what she is, poor child. Any girl with health and strength is regarded as a natural enemy, and then Miss Whittingham has had charge of Amy, which has prejudiced her against her.'

'In what way?'

She became suddenly evasive. 'Oh, I don't know . . . but I'm glad Amy is to stay with the Ulsbornes for a time. It is best for her to be out of this house. I did wrong to take her in the first place.'

'You acted out of kindness, Aunt Anna.'

'Did I?' She looked at him strangely and muttered something that he could not catch about one's sins coming home to roost, and then she finished her pretence at a breakfast and went back to her daughter.

Gradually the household settled down to a new routine.

Pouncer's married sister came to collect her belongings and Catherine moved to the empty room next to Mrs. Ravensbourne's, to be summoned night or day at a moment's notice, even if she was trying to catch up on a night's sleep. She had the idea, however, that Mrs. Ravensbourne was not to blame for this lack of consideration: it was Edith who was exerting an invalid's privilege of being humoured.

But as she grew stronger and more irritable, Mrs. Ravensbourne was with her for most of the day, and Catherine was employed on other things. She was sent downstairs to interview Cook and to bring back a menu for Mrs. Ravensbourne's perusal, and was sent back again with it completely rewritten. She gave orders to the tradespeople and arranged Edith's flowers and made her bed, and brought up trays of food while her own got cold on the dining-room table, because schoolroom meals were now things of the past, and Mrs. Ravensbourne had her own meals with Edith.

And as the pattern of their lives altered, Mrs. Ravensbourne found that she was able to rely more and more upon the calm, quiet young woman who took offence at nothing, and was as ready to undertake Maggie's duties as Pouncer's. She even discovered an unaccustomed sense of comfort in the girl's company, and had a word or two of praise for her when Edith scolded.

William Ravensbourne stayed a week before returning to Yorkshire, spending his days in Brighton and his nights in Worthing. Every morning before he came to see his aunt he paid a visit to his daughter, who had come back to Brunswick Square with her cousins, and he was able to report to Catherine on her health and conduct.

The first morning after their return to Brunswick Square Amy had immediately asked after her dear Catherine. 'I do hope Edith gets better soon,' she said anxiously, 'so that I can go back to her.'

'You wouldn't like to stay with your cousins for good, then?' asked her father, and saw her look at him suspiciously, as if she were questioning what lay beneath the question.

'Catherine isn't going to leave me for Edith, is she?' she asked apprehensively. 'She can't do that . . . she promised she would never leave me.'

'No, of course not.' He saw the fright in her eyes and took her hand consolingly. 'She is only with Edith while she is so ill. Directly she is better you will have her back again.' He paused before adding curiously, 'Is she so important to you?'

Amy nodded gravely. 'A person has to have somebody all to themselves,' she explained. 'When you have nobody but yourself it's like living in a bare room with only a chair and a table in it—like my schoolroom was until Catherine made it pretty with her things. I don't mind *lending* her to Edith as long as she promises to get better soon, but I can't *give* her to her . . . it wouldn't be fair.' Her lips quivered and he tried belatedly to make amends.

'Then you shall have her back again, and perhaps some day you and Miss Whittingham will have a home of your own.'

Her face lit up. 'When?' she asked eagerly. 'When can we have it? Soon? And where is it to be?'

'Not so fast, young woman! There are a lot of things to be arranged, and poor Edith has got to get well first.' But although he laughed his arm went round his daughter's slight shoulders in an unaccustomed caress. 'I promise you this, though, directly it is possible I will buy a house for you.'

She turned her head, staring at him intently as if reading his thoughts, and then, assured that he was speaking the truth, she leaned forward and kissed his cheek. 'Thank you,' she said. 'You are very kind.'

He might have been a tradesman who had served her over the counter, so distant was her manner: it had in it the aloof dignity that had been her mother's, and he knew then with a stab of the old pain that if he wanted to win his daughter's love he would have to work hard and patiently. Amy was not a child to be bribed or coaxed into loving. She would either give her heart completely or she would keep it to herself.

He left her with a mixture of feelings in which grief for the spoilt years and regret for his long neglect of her were uppermost in his mind, and he determined to get his business in Yorkshire finished as soon as possible so that he could get back to her.

*   *   *

It was Edith who suggested one day that Catherine should play to her. It was a wet afternoon and Mrs. Ravensbourne had gone out alone in the closed carriage for her airing.

'You know I hate stuffy carriages,' Edith said petulantly

when she was asked if she wouldn't accompany her. 'The smell of the leather and the horses makes my head ache. If I can't go in an open carriage I won't go at all.'

'Then you had better stay here with Catherine,' said Mrs. Ravensbourne good-humouredly. A few weeks ago they would never have believed how easily they could slip into using her Christian name. 'She can disentangle those embroidery silks for you. My eyes aren't good enough, and my fingers haven't the patience for it.'

'Give them to me,' said Catherine, smiling. She took the wad of silks to the window and began sorting out the different colours from the tangled heap in her lap, and she had been at it for some time when Edith said in a plaintive voice:

'Oh dear, how bored I am! Can't you talk to me . . . or play the piano?'

'It depends which you prefer, my conversation or the music.'

'Oh, the music would be better, of course,' said Edith, and then wanted to know what Catherine was laughing at.

'I was thinking that it would be hard to grow conceited in this house,' she said.

Grudgingly Edith smiled too, and Catherine thought how much prettier she was when she forgot to frown. She said placatingly, 'I didn't mean to be rude, but if you will play the piano you have my full permission to be as conceited as you like, because I can't play it at all!'

'Very well.' Catherine put down the silks carefully on the window-seat and seated herself at the piano. 'What would you like me to play?'

Edith stared. 'But you haven't any music!'

'I don't need it for some things. Do you like Chopin, or Handel or Beethoven? Or would you prefer something light and gay—a song from one of Gilbert and Sullivan's operas?'

'No . . . not that!' Edith spoke quickly and shrinkingly, her eyes hurt and protesting as if the operas held painful memories. 'Beethoven, I think . . . the Moonlight Sonata.'

Catherine plunged into her memory and began to play, her fingers, stiff at first through lack of practice, soon finding their old way of caressing the keys, her touch that of one who loved the instrument she was playing, and Edith listened without interruption. It seemed that for once she had forgotten that she must be the centre of attraction, and glad that they had hit on something that would amuse her, Catherine gave way to the joy of playing again, and became so absorbed in the music that she did not see Mrs. Ravensbourne slip into the room unnoticed behind her.

'Bravo!' she cried as she finished. 'I didn't know we had such a talented musician in our midst, did you, Edith?' Then her voice changed. 'Why, Edith, you are crying! ... What is the matter, child?'

'Nothing. Go away and leave me alone. I want to speak to Catherine.'

Mrs. Ravensbourne hesitated and then went away reluctantly, while Catherine left the piano and knelt down by the sofa.

'What is the matter, dear?' she asked gently, taking the invalid's hand. 'Did I hurt you with my playing?'

'No ... but it reminded me of myself. Those two movements, the first so dreamy and quiet, the second fiery and untamed ... It was like me ... and I can't help it. I don't mean to do the things I do or to say the things I say ... It's as if there were two people inside me, one wanting to be loving and kind, the other ready to hurt and destroy ... Why am I like this? Why should I be split in halves? Other people aren't ... What is the matter with me, Catherine?'

'You are tired, my love, and the music has upset you.' But as Edith clung to her, weeping, Catherine looked with dismay into the future and saw the divided path ahead and did not know which way she could tread with safety.

Edith and Amy, both turned to her for help and comfort and relied on her for all she had to give, and yet which of them needed her most? She could not break her promise to the child, but how was she to stop Edith from becoming more and more dependent on her?

The weeks went by so quickly that it surprised her one day to discover that it was over a month since she had heard from Bella. When her sister's letter came she put it aside to read when she was in bed that night, and then she did not know whether to laugh or to cry over its closely written pages. *My dearest*, Bella began, *I don't know what you will say to my news, but Anthony and I are engaged to be married* ...

Catherine read no more than the first paragraph. She knew what the rest of the letter would be like: the delight of the Trantams, and 'Aunt Sarah' in particular, who would be able to congratulate herself on planning the whole thing, the messages from Anthony, who would feel bound to make some sort of apology for having preferred her sister after all his protestations to herself, the description of Bella's engagement ring, and the wedding plans. Nothing would have been forgotten, and all of it would come from a world that now seemed more alien to her than any other.

She put the letter away, intending to write the next day to congratulate Bella and Anthony, but when the morning came there was no time in which to compose a suitable message to the happy pair. And yet write she must. In the end she compromised by sending a telegram: *Delighted with your news. Love and blessings to you both, Kate.*

As she left the post office she thanked heaven for the invention of the telegraph. It saved much worry and heartache and hard work.

She went back to Mecklinburgh Square to help Edith to dress before giving her a piano lesson. Having refused to learn all her life, she was now anxious to know all that Catherine could teach her: she was looking better and brighter than she had done for a long time, and she said she would put on a new blouse that had recently come from Mrs. Westcott.

'It is in the top drawer of the chest in my dressing-room,' she said as Catherine went to get it for her.

Catherine opened the drawer and found the blouse between layers of tissue paper, and then suddenly, as she was about to take it out, her hands stopped short.

The drawer was flooded with scent, a sweet, heady, familiar perfume, that had leaked from a small unstoppered cut-glass bottle tucked away at the back and wrapped up in a little bundle of torn lace and ribbon: her own missing bottle of attar of roses.

14

The holiday season had now reached its peak, and every day, including Sundays, excursion trains brought thousands of trippers into the town and thronging down to the beach. Edith refused to go out in the bath-chair that her mother hired for her: she said she would not be pressed on and stared at by crowds of people.

She grew tired of her piano lessons and bored with her embroidery, and seemed to find most pleasure in her evening stroll with Catherine in the square gardens. Their conversation, however, always came round to one subject, and every time it was mentioned Edith complained of weakness and leant on Catherine's arm for support. The Ulsbornes were leaving Brighton in September, and unless they took Amy with them the child must come back to Mecklinburgh Square.

'Let her come back, then!' said Edith one evening, after a more heated argument than usual. 'Mother can get another governess for her. *You* will stay with me now!'

Once more Catherine pointed out that she had been engaged as Amy's governess, and that when the child returned she must resume that duty. 'You know I must, Edith,' she protested. 'I promised Amy I would not leave her.'

'You shouldn't have promised, then!' Edith began to shake. 'You are upsetting me. My heart is banging like a hammer!'

'Then let's sit down and talk of something else.'

'I'd be all right if you'd stay with me.' Edith shot a sly glance at her. 'It's too bad of you to let me get used to you and then threaten to abandon me for that wretched child. I've always hated her and now I hate her more than ever.'

'But I'm not abandoning you yet.' Catherine refused to be

drawn into any more argument. 'And it's silly to say that you hate people, because I'm sure you don't. Look at the light on the sea! Isn't it lovely? We'll bring our sketching things tomorrow if it is as fine as this . . .'

And then towards the end of August William Ravensbourne returned to Brighton and called one morning with tickets for an orchestral concert at the Pier Pavilion that night.

'Aunt Anna said you were learning music with Miss Whittingham,' he told Edith, 'and so I bought four tickets, so that we can take her with us. You are stronger now and an outing would do you good.'

'No.' Edith drew back. 'I had a bad night and I'm tired. I shall be tired all day and fit for nothing by tonight. I don't want to go to any stupid concert.'

'Then Catherine shall go with Will and I'll stay with you, dear,' said her mother placidly. 'I will send Albert across to Mrs. Wainwright to ask her if she will act as chaperon.'

Catherine felt a moment of shrinking which she quickly suppressed. Vulgar and loud-voiced as Mrs. Wainwright was, she would no doubt enjoy the music, and she would be glad of her company: she had no desire to spend an evening alone with Ravensbourne before he went back to his accommodating Yorkshire friend in Worthing.

'It's the first time I've heard of a governess needing a chaperon,' said Edith disagreeably. She was in one of her bad, difficult moods.

'Let me stay with her, Mrs. Ravensbourne,' said Catherine urgently. 'It will be much better. You will be free then to go out with your nephew.'

But this did not please Edith either.

'I don't want you or Mother,' she said. 'The maids are in, aren't they? Why should I need anyone to keep me company?'

Her mother sat down beside her and took her hand.

'But you are not getting rid of me, my love,' she said firmly. 'Because I am staying with you.'

Finally it was settled that Catherine should go, the note was sent across the square, and the invitation accepted, and after an early meal that evening she went to get dressed.

She found it a little difficult to select a dress that would be simple enough to be in keeping with her position in the household, and yet grand enough for Mrs. Wainwright. In the end she chose a grey silk, with a rose-pink velvet belt and full sleeves, and she tied a narrow black velvet ribbon round her throat in place of a necklace. She added long white gloves, picked up a black lace scarf and fan, and went into Edith's room for Mrs. Ravensbourne's approval.

'That is a very pretty dress, Catherine,' she said graciously. 'Not in the latest fashion, of course, but I suppose it is one you have had for some time?'

'It was made for me two summers ago,' said Catherine. She spared a nostalgic thought for those summer evenings at Grey Ladies, when she had strolled on the terrace and under the old trees on the lawns with Anthony, the grey silk of her dress gleaming in the shadows, and his eyes searching for hers in the dusk.

'I don't like it,' said Edith sharply. 'I had one that colour once, but it was much prettier. And that ribbon round your neck makes you look so old.'

'I think it is very becoming,' said Mrs. Ravensbourne. 'And I'm glad you are taking a fan with you. The Pier Pavilion can get very warm on a summer night.'

Catherine tried to win a smile from Edith before she left. 'Won't you go instead of me?' she pleaded. 'There is still time to get you ready before your cousin comes.'

'I will *not* go!' Edith glared at her. 'I *hate* concerts!'

Catherine gave it up and said a quiet good night to Mrs. Ravensbourne. 'There is no need for any of the servants to wait up for me. I will bolt the front door when I come in.'

'My servants will do as they're told,' said Mrs. Ravensbourne crisply. 'And there will be biscuits and wine in the dining-room in case Mr. Ravensbourne likes to have something before he returns to Worthing.'

'Thank you.' The mention of Worthing took the smile from Catherine's eyes. 'I will tell him that it is there.'

'Quite the grand lady tonight, aren't you?' jeered Edith from her sofa, her eyes bright and her cheeks flushed. 'The sooner Amy comes back and you start being her governess again the better, otherwise we'll have you setting your cap at poor Will!'

Catherine stood still for a moment by the door and then she said: 'I will fetch Amy tomorrow, Edith. I shall be glad to have her back.' And she went out, closing the door gently behind her.

'Edith!' Mrs. Ravensbourne was reproachful. 'How can you

say such things to Catherine after all her goodness to you? I think sometimes you are the most ungrateful girl that ever lived!'

'I hate her!' Edith's voice rose excitedly. 'And I won't have her marry Will.'

'Who said she was going to marry Will? And if she did it might be no bad thing.' Her mother sounded tired and depressed. 'If you are over your tantrums I'll help you into bed.'

'I want help from nobody. I can get myself to bed.'

'I am glad to hear it. I think I heard the carriage, and I'll go and have a word with Mrs. Wainwright before they go.' Mrs. Ravensbourne went away, leaving her daughter alone, and to Edith it seemed that the big room was suddenly full of people.

She could see Amy, putting a timid white face round the door, and William, stiff and yet kind, asking her how she was, and Mary, laughing at her behind her back and leaving her to sit out the dances alone while she went by, waltzing like a feather in the arms of John Tempest, and John Tempest himself with those steely eyes that never grew warm but only looked beyond her to the money that would be hers when they married, and last of all Catherine, sitting at the piano playing in the dusk ... Catherine rubbing her hands, washing her face, bringing food trays to her with a gay, 'Now eat all this up before I go!' Catherine, walking with her along the front, reading to her in the square, sketching with her there, and finishing pieces of embroidery that she had grown tired of with so much more patience and skill than she possessed ... Catherine, whom she had grown to love ... or was it hate that she felt for her most?

Her head ached and she grew confused. The murmur of voices in the hall became louder and she heard Will laugh, and then the front door closed and her mother came back up the stairs.

Up the stairs ... Her thoughts turned to the attic schoolroom at the top of the house, with Catherine's pictures on the walls and her gay cushions on the chairs and curtains at the window, and the many books on the shelves. On that Sunday afternoon when she had first taken Amy round to Brunswick Square Edith had climbed the stairs to see it for herself and she had known at once in its atmosphere of cosy warmth the close companionship that must exist between Mary's child and her governess.

It was stupid of her to forget it in discovering a new affection for this false friend. 'I will fetch Amy tomorrow,' she said only a few minutes ago, standing by the door over there, her face full of contempt. 'I will be glad to have her back.' And in recalling that all the affection she had for Catherine died, and only hate was left, taking possession of her heart and telling her what to do.

She lay back and closed her eyes, and Mrs. Ravensbourne, looking in, thought she was asleep, and, reassured, went away thankfully to have her dinner.

*   *   *

Once the door of Number Five had closed behind them and she was driving away with William and Mrs. Wainwright, Catherine began to enjoy her evening. The lady had put on all her jewels in honour of the occasion and sparkled so much that she looked as if she might have been first dipped in treacle and then rolled in diamonds. But once she got over her desire to impress Catherine she was kind enough, and during the concert she explained to her some of the more ambitious pieces played by the orchestra.

'That was from *Tannhäuser*, dear,' she said once from behind her large feather fan. 'An opera by Wagner—a German composer. I like Puccini best. Very gay, the Puccini music. Have you ever been to the opera, dear?'

Catherine said she had, and was sorry because Mrs. Wainwright looked so put out, and changed the subject by asking her if she liked going to the play. Mrs. Wainwright said there was nothing like a good play. She and her late lamented Mr. Wainwright went to see a play by that naughty Oscar Wilde that was very amusing, something about a fan. Yes, that was it, dear, *Lady Windermere's Fan*. Mr. W. thought it very comic —very comic indeed. That was when they were in London on one of Mr. W.'s business trips. She wouldn't let him go alone, because you never knew what a gentleman might get up to, did you, dear?

Catherine listened and smiled assent, being only required to put in a word now and then, while William sat glumly on the lady's other side, staring at his programme and occasionally raising his eyes to stare at his aunt's friend as if wondering how one woman could say so many stupid things in so short a time. They were not relieved of her presence until the interval, when he got up abruptly and suggested they should go outside for a breath of air. It was a very hot night, but the sky was overcast and dark, and Mrs. Wainwright preferred to stay where she was.

'The worst of being stout is that once you get into a comfortable seat you don't want to get out of it again,' she told her companions. 'But you go with Mr. R., Miss Whittingham. He'll prefer your company to mine, I'm sure!'

So William gave Catherine his arm and they joined those of the audience who were also taking a turn along the parade.

'It feels as if there is a storm brewing,' she remarked. The street lamps and the lighted windows of the big hotels were strung along the front like jewels set out on black velvet. 'There is not a star to be seen.'

'No.' He added stiffly, 'I'm sorry we had to have Mrs. Wainwright with us, but I suppose, as my aunt could not leave Edith, it wouldn't have been proper for you to come by yourself.'

'Your aunt was very kind in finding me a chaperon, although I will admit that Edith scarcely thought a governess needed one.'

He did not laugh. He was silent for a long moment and then he said quietly, 'But I think it is some time now since Aunt Anna thought of you as a governess.'

'Yet that was what I was engaged for, and that is what I hope to return to as soon as it is possible.' As he did not reply she went on: 'Edith is getting tired of me. I have been quite unable to please her lately and I shall be glad to have Amy home. I feel I have neglected her far too long for a spoilt, wilful young woman, who uses her ill-health as a means for getting her own way.'

'Aren't you being a little hard on her? She is far from strong.'

'She is a great deal stronger than she appears to be. She told me once that she had a split personality, and this last week I have seen it for myself. She seems to wish to be loved, and yet she will repay any demonstration of affection with an intense and rather terrible hatred. One moment she wants to build up a friendship, and the next she sets out to destroy it.' She glanced up at his grave face in the light of a lamp. 'I may be wrong . . . I hope I am. You may put it down to nervous fancy, or the storm in the air tonight.'

'No, I don't think you are altogether wrong. I haven't understood Edith properly myself for a long time now. And that is why I am determined to buy a house. I want to take on the responsibility of a parent, and to install Amy in her own home, with you as her companion and friend. I know you are young to take such an establishment on your shoulders, but housekeepers and servants can be engaged, and if you would like your sister to live with you she would be very welcome.'

'You are very good.' Catherine did not quite know what to say. 'But my sister is getting married shortly.'

'Have you any other female relative, then, who would like to be with you, and whose company you would welcome?'

'Well, there is Aunt Emily—my mother's unmarried sister. She would be delighted to come, and I would be as glad to have her. I think too that she and Amy would get along famously, because she acted as a mother to Bella and myself for years.'

'Then that settles it.' He sounded relieved. 'We will go on as we are for a few more weeks while I look for a suitable house, and when I have found it I will have your aunt's name and address, so that you and she and Amy may move in when the time comes.'

The interval was nearly over and the audience was returning to the lighted doorway of the Pier Pavilion. As they joined the others he looked from the slender hand on his sleeve to her thoughtful eyes. 'I take it I may depend on you?' he said.

She seemed surprised that he should question it. 'But of course!'

The thought of her aunt being freed from the unhappy servitude of Putney, and little Amy in her own home at last, brought a flush to her cheeks and a light to her eyes as she returned to her seat, and Mrs. Wainwright did not fail to comment on it.

'Now what has Mr. Ravensbourne been saying that has made you look so pretty?' she asked. 'No, don't tell me! I can guess! I know what gentlemen are like when they get a young lady out under the stars.'

'But there aren't any stars tonight,' said Catherine quickly, and was annoyed to catch a droll expression in William's eyes for a moment as if he would have liked to laugh.

'But those lamps on the parade are just as good!' said Mrs. Wainwright archly. 'Don't tell me they aren't!'

Setting her cap at Will, flirting with Mr. R. on the parade, really, thought Catherine angrily, this was a bit too much! Didn't Mrs. Wainwright know about the Yorkshire widow in Worthing? She did not look his way again and confined her eyes to the orchestra and the programme until the concert ended and they were free to go home.

The stuffiness of the concert room and the airlessness of the night had given her a headache, and after they had dropped Mrs. Wainwright at her house she was relieved when William Ravensbourne refused to come in and sample the refreshment that had been left out for him.

'You look tired,' he said. 'I will not keep you up any longer. Good night, Miss Whittingham.'

She tried to make amends for her ungraciousness. 'Thank you for a very pleasant evening,' she said. 'I enjoyed it very much indeed.'

'The pleasure was mine,' he said almost coldly, and as Maggie opened the door for her he went back to the waiting carriage and drove off in it without another glance, obviously impatient to catch his train back to Worthing.

Catherine felt depressed as she went upstairs to bed, followed by a yawning Maggie.

'Do you want unhooking, miss?' she asked. 'The mistress said I was to help you when you came in.'

'Thank you, Maggie, but I can get out of this dress by myself. You go off to bed now—you look half asleep.'

'It's a lovely dress, miss,' said Maggie admiringly. 'And it suits you a treat. I don't suppose there was another young lady there half as beautiful as you were tonight.'

'Oh, Maggie, you'll make me conceited if you talk like that!' But the unexpected praise was almost unbearably sweet, all the same, and as they came to Catherine's door she stood there for a moment smiling at the girl. 'Good night . . . and thank you for waiting up!'

Maggie vanished down the corridor and Catherine went into her room and got undressed and into bed.

But as she blew out her candle and lay down in the oppressive darkness her thoughts went back to all the little details of the evening, and dominating them all was the dark, brooding face of William Ravensbourne. She saw again and again the inscrutable expression in his eyes as they had rested on her from time to time during the concert, and she could hear his cold, unemotional voice when he said good night.

Nobody could say that his interest in her was other than that of an employer giving his child's governess a treat, and how quick he had been to take up her criticism of Edith. She turned over in bed and told herself wryly: 'I cannot seem to remember that I'm only a paid servant here. The slightest sign of patronage or ordinary kindness and I start behaving like a fine lady, giving unasked opinions and forgetting that I'm speaking of my betters!'

The storm broke in a sudden rumble of thunder over the square, banishing sleep completely. She was tired and yet she was wide awake, listening to the rain that beat on her windows, and the sharp gusts of wind that made them creak and groan. The wind blew down the passage outside from the open window over the stairs, and rattled her door, as if unseen fingers were trying it to see if it were locked.

She lay still in Pouncer's narrow bed, listening to the rage and fury of the elements, the room lit every now and then by flashes of sheet lightning, and she thought of the sea and those that sailed on it, and wondered if Amy were frightened in Brunswick Square, and if Miss Mattison would go to her if she were. During a lull in the noise outside she thought footsteps moved away down the corridor, and there came the faint, distant scroop of a baize door, and if Edith had been kinder when they parted that evening she would have got up to see if she felt ill. But Edith's ingratitude had been building up into a formidable barrier between them, and she had no wish to bring fresh fury on her head at that time of night. So she turned over and pulled the bedclothes over her head, and as the storm died down she went to sleep.

It was early in the morning when she was awakened by an urgent knocking on her door.

'Miss Whittingham!' Maggie's voice, low-pitched and frightened, implored her to wake up. 'Can you come up to the schoolroom at once, please?'

Catherine unlocked her door and drew the girl into her room. 'Maggie dear! What is the matter?' She spoke in a whisper so that she should not disturb Mrs. Ravensbourne next door, but although she was only half awake she could see that the maid looked scared to death.

'Oh, Miss Whittingham!' Maggie began to cry softly, rubbing the backs of her hands into her eyes like a child. 'It's horrible ... I've never seen anything like it ... for anybody to be so wicked and so cruel.'

Catherine did not wait for any further explanations. Without stopping for dressing-gown or slippers she sped away down the corridor barefoot and in her nightdress, and up the two flights of stairs, and then along the corridor in the nursery floor to the last baize door that shut off the wooden staircase to the attics.

It was not until she came to the garret schoolroom that she came to an abrupt halt, as appalled as Maggie by what she saw.

Amy's lesson books had been taken from the cupboard and the pages torn out and blotted with ink. The story books on the shelves had disappeared: they were found later in a sodden heap on the balcony below the window, having been exposed to the rain all night, but the bindings of many had been ripped off first and flung into the grate. The cushions on the chairs were slashed, the feathers scattered, the curtains hung in tatters, the glass in the pictures was smashed, the frames reduced to matchwood, and the white sheepskin rug in front of the fireplace was splashed with red and black ink. It was a scene of such wanton destruction that at first sight it looked as if some wild animal had been let loose in it, and in the midst of it was a slight figure in a pale blue wrapper, sitting motionless at the table with her head on her spread-out arms, and in her clenched hands a little carved sandalwood box.

15

'I heard the window banging,' said Maggie. 'I thought it was queer, because I shut it last night in case of rain. So I came up here and this is what I found. Is she . . . dead, miss?'

Catherine bent over Edith and touched her cheek: its waxy pallor and icy coldness sent a chill to her heart.

'Send Albert for the doctor,' she said. 'Tell him to run all the way. And then go and wake your mistress and say that Miss Edith has been taken ill up here, and will she please come?'

Her orders, given with an authority and calm she was far from feeling, did much to steady Maggie. She raced away and in a very little while Mrs. Ravensbourne came, with a crimson flannel dressing-gown over her voluminous nightgown and her fringe still in curlers.

'I knew something like this would happen,' she said, going to her daughter and shaking her shoulder gently. 'She hated the thought of Amy coming back, and yet she wanted her here, to torment her because of what Mary did to her.' She stooped lower to the motionless figure lying across the table. 'Edith, my love, come down to your room. It's cold up here, and your hands are like ice.'

As she waited for a movement that did not come she glanced about her and seemed as blind to the devastation in the room as she was to the gravity of her daughter's condition. 'It's a bad heart attack,' she said reassuringly. 'It's no more than that, but I'm glad you've sent for the doctor. She will recover directly we can get her downstairs. Go and fetch the smelling salts.'

Catherine came back with the salts and a blanket which she wrapped round Edith while Mrs. Ravensbourne held the little bottle under her nose.

'She's so still,' she complained. 'I've never known her as still as this before, but there's nothing to be alarmed about. She has frightened me times without number, getting off on her own like this and exciting herself and then suddenly collapsing. I'll sit here with her while you get dressed.'

Catherine left her and dressed as quickly as her shaking fingers would allow: she was just hooking up her skirt when the doctor came. She took him up to the schoolroom, where he examined Edith and told her mother as gently as he could that her daughter was dead.

Mrs. Ravensbourne refused to believe him, and told him not to be a fool, and Catherine had only a confused recollection of what happened after that. She remembered calling Maggie and Cook, and getting their mistress downstairs and into a chair by a hastily lighted fire because she was shaking all over as if she were cold. She remembered the doctor and Albert bringing Edith's body down to her room, and she remembered writing out a telegram to William Ravensbourne in Worthing. The address in particular stamped itself on her mind: *C/o Mrs. Elizabeth Huggins, Mon Repos, Marine Parade.* As she wrote it out she could see in her mind's eye a tall, narrow villa fronting on to the sea, with discreetly curtained windows, and a small general servant taking the yellow envelope from the telegraph boy and running with it to the accommodating widow and her male companion.

It was just after twelve when Ravensbourne arrived and asked to see her, and as she came down into the hall he was again impressed by her dignity and calm bearing in that house of shadows.

'This is a terrible business, Miss Whittingham,' he said. 'How is my aunt?'

'The doctor has given her a sleeping draught and I have tucked her up on the sofa in the drawing-room. We are hoping she will sleep for a time, but the shock has been considerable.'

'Of course. How did it happen? Did Edith die in her sleep?'

'No. Maggie found her early this morning up in the school-room.'

'In the schoolroom?' He was astonished. 'What was she doing there?'

She hesitated before she said quietly, 'I think perhaps you had better come and see.'

He glanced at her quickly, and then followed her without question to the top of the house and stood surveying the scene of destruction in grim silence.

'I don't know why she did it,' said Catherine gently. 'But it may have been because I told her before I went out last evening that I would be glad to bring Amy back here as soon as possible. She was very jealous of my affection for the child.'

'She hated Amy.' He went to the table and picked up the sandalwood box. 'Is this yours?'

'No, it belongs to Amy.' She told him about the Chesters' visit and how the box had come into their hands through Albert, and that she had kept it for Amy in her trunk until it disappeared one afternoon while they were out. 'I have not seen it since,' she added, 'until I saw it in Edith's hands this morning.'

He looked at it closely, examining the silver initials on the lid with distaste, and then he fitted the key in the lock and opened it. The letter and documents and the cotton bag of glass beads were still there, and he picked up the letter with an air of shrinking dislike foreign to his strong nature.

'Lady Ulsborne thought the letter might be from Amy's mother,' she told him uncertainly.

'Lady Ulsborne was right.' He weighed the letter in his hand and then said harshly, 'I think I'd better read this.'

He broke the seal and sat down at the table while Catherine

walked to the window and examined the books that Albert had rescued from the balcony and spread out on the floor to dry. As she stood them up on end, trying to separate the soaked pages, behind her William Ravensbourne studied the letter, his only sign of emotion being the tightening of a muscle in his cheek as he read. Presently he replaced it in the envelope and turned his attention to the documents with the detachment he might have given to business contracts of his own, and finally he emptied the bag of beads into his hand and examined them too. Then he called Catherine over to him.

'I am going to burn this letter, Miss Whittingham,' he said evenly. 'And I want you to be a witness to it. Its contents would only hurt a young woman of twenty-one, and it would serve no useful purpose in being kept for Amy to read. My wife appeared to think when she wrote it that her conduct would be excused in her daughter's eyes if she gave the full reasons why she married me and afterwards left me for Tempest, but they are scarcely reasons that everyone would appreciate.' He stared past her at the tattered curtains and the smashed pictures without seeing them.

He had always hoped against hope that Mary would one day get tired of Tempest and come back to him. He had never realized until today how much she had hated him. But then he had never understood her: he had only been able to love her, and his love was not enough.

Catherine wished she could say something that would take the stricken look from his face, but he seemed to have forgotten her, and presently he went on:

'These documents are share certificates, of one thousand pounds each, in a South African diamond-mine. The cotton bag appears to contain uncut diamonds, and she expresses the wish in her letter that both shares and diamonds should be Amy's. As she died intestate, however, by law they belong to me, which is a good thing, as Amy need know nothing about them. When I have discovered the value of the shares and the stones I will sell the lot and give the proceeds to a hospital, and with the equivalent in cash I will start an account for Amy to inherit when she is twenty-one. In the meantime perhaps you will refrain from telling her that the box has been found.'

'I won't say a word, Mr. Ravensbourne. If nobody reminds her of it she is not likely to remember it herself.'

'Thank you.' He put the letter in the empty grate and set it alight and watched it burn. It was curious, he thought, how one could make allowances for a person for years because one cared for them so deeply, and then suddenly one could make allowances no more.

Catherine, watching the curling ash, saw the name *Mary Ravensbourne* clearly and boldly in black on grey before it flickered out and died, and as it did so Ravensbourne put his foot on it and crushed it into powder. As she saw his face in that moment it came to her that the natives who had murdered his wife out in Africa had not killed her more completely than she had killed herself in his eyes by that letter.

She longed to help him, but she knew he would not thank her for any expression of sympathy. You did not say you were sorry for somebody who had been mortally hurt. All she could find to say was, 'Is there anything I can do?'

'Yes, there is.' He turned his back on the grate and surveyed the ruined room frowningly. 'I am sorry about this, but I will try to replace these things in time, if you will be so good as to furnish me with a list of everything that has been spoilt. I must stay here with my aunt until the funeral is over: there are business matters to be settled and she has no one else to depend on. But she will not want Amy back, and I would like you to pack your things today, if you please, so that you will be ready to leave the house tomorrow.'

'Tomorrow?' She was not accustomed to such abrupt orders and his frown deepened.

'I will send a note by Albert to Lady Ulsborne's governess asking her to have Amy ready for you tomorrow morning, so that you can call for her directly after breakfast and take her with you to Worthing. I have an old friend there who will look after you both until I can make more permanent arrangements.'

Catherine's heart sank. It appeared that the Yorkshire widow was to accommodate him still further: but perhaps now he was free he planned to marry her, and that was why he was anxious for her to become acquainted with his daughter. As this thought crossed her mind he collected the papers on the table and packed them away neatly in the box with the diamonds.

'Am I asking too much of you?' he asked, as she stood there motionless. 'Can you not do your packing in time?'

'I can do it easily, Mr. Ravensbourne.' She roused herself and tried to be as businesslike as he was. 'You may leave Amy to me. I will look after her.'

'I know that.' He hesitated for a moment, as if he would like to say more and then he turned abruptly to the stairs. 'For God's sake let's get out of this wretched room!' he exclaimed, and leaving Catherine to her packing he went on down to his aunt.

Much as she disliked the idea of being entertained by his Mrs. Huggins in Worthing, Catherine knew that she could serve him best by carrying out his orders. Her boxes were ready long before evening, but she did not see Mrs. Ravensbourne or her nephew again that day. Only Maggie was allowed in her mistress's room, and Catherine wrote a little note of sympathy, thanks and goodbye, to be given to her after her cab had left in the morning. When the moment of departure came only Maggie and Albert were there to see her off, and not a curtain moved at the windows as the cab turned out of the square: the house was as cold and inhospitable as it had been on the day she arrived, and the events of that Jubilee summer might have been only a dream.

But her welcome in Brunswick Square made up for it. Here she was greeted rapturously by Amy, who was waiting and ready and far too delighted at being with her dear Catherine again to be heart-broken at leaving her cousins.

At Brighton station, however, a surprise awaited them: Ravensbourne was there to conduct them to Worthing in person before moving into his aunt's house for a time, and he forestalled Amy's fire of questions by presenting her with a small black dog by the name of Rip.

'She has done nothing but talk about Glossy every time I've been to see her lately,' he told Catherine as their train started off. 'I was determined that whatever the South can do Yorkshire can do better, and fortunately Mrs. Huggins doesn't object to having a dog in her rooms.'

'Is that where we are going?' asked Amy. 'To Mrs. Huggins? What is she like?'

He seemed to find this hard to answer. 'She is a Yorkshire woman, but I could not tell you if she is handsome or ugly, because she is a friend, and all my friends have nice faces.'

'Is she very old?'

He laughed. 'Miss Whittingham will tell you that you must never ask questions about a lady's age. I should say that Mrs. Huggins is as old as she feels.'

Catherine smiled faintly and turned her attention to the hills beyond the town, where sunshine was making patches among the shadows in the folds of the Downs. She felt she knew quite enough about Elizabeth Huggins already, and she had little interest in the lady, although when a little while later the train approached Worthing she would have given almost anything to be back in their garret schoolroom in Mecklinburgh Square.

But the engine came to a groaning halt, and they were out on the platform much too soon, and walking into the station yard, where among a row of cabs waiting to be hired, one was standing ready for them.

William Ravensbourne seemed to be well known in the little country station. Porters ran to fetch the luggage, and the cabby touched his hat and did not need to be told anything beyond 'The Marine Parade as usual, driver,' before moving off.

Catherine found herself answering Amy's questions at random as they made their slow way towards the front. The large houses standing back in their pleasant gardens might have been rows of slum cottages from all the interest she could find in them, and she could only think of their impending arrival with a nervous dread that increased every moment.

The front was much simpler than that of Brighton, with the beach reaching up to the parade and tossing its pebbles across it on to the road. The air was fresh with the smell of seaweed and salt, but the front itself was far too short for the apprehensive Miss Whittingham.

In no time at all they were stopping outside a large double-fronted house, its stucco front painted a light green, with 'Mon Repos' in raised white letters on the fanlight over the front door, and as the cab came to a standstill a woman came hurrying out on to the steps as if she had been watching for them. A grey-haired, middle-aged woman, with an apron tied over her black dress, who reached the carriage door before Ravensbourne could get to it.

'Well, Eliza,' he said. 'Here we are . . . and this is my daughter.'

She did not wait to hear any more, but she lifted Amy down and kissed her heartily and exclaimed, 'Eh, Mr. William, she's the very image of you!' before taking her hand and leading her into the house.

He was left to assist Catherine and little Rip out of the cab, and as she took the little dog under her arm she was glad that there was no occasion for her to speak. She was shocked into silence as she recalled Helen Ulsborne's description of Mr. Ravensbourne's Yorkshire widow, and her own credulity. She might have known that the vulgar, over-dressed female of Lady Ulsborne's imagination would scarcely appeal to his taste, and she was so vexed with herself for having believed half of it that he had to repeat what he had to say twice before she heard him.

'I was saying that I don't think you will find this house uncomfortable,' he told her patiently, evidently guessing that General Whittingham's daughters were not accustomed to staying in boarding houses. 'Eliza has set aside two bedrooms and a large sitting-room for your use on the first floor. They are bright, cheerful rooms: I asked particularly that they should look over the sea. Eliza's cooking is excellent, by the way: I wouldn't have been such a frequent lodger of hers if it hadn't been. After my business trips abroad Mon Repos has been a very comfortable half-way house between Southampton and Yorkshire.'

She could understand him preferring it to his aunt's house in Brighton: the comfort there was nil, and the cooking at times abominable.

'You'll wait for a bite to eat before you go?' asked Mrs. Huggins anxiously. 'You don't spare yourself a mite, I know, but the dinner's all ready to go upstairs.'

'No, I won't wait for it, thank you, Eliza. My aunt expects me back.' His luggage was in the hall, waiting to go with him in the cab, and he summoned the cabby to fetch it. 'But before I go,' he added, 'I'll just have a word with that lad of yours.' He opened the door into a small room to the right where a boy of nineteen was sitting with a rug over his knees, mending a pair of boots. 'Well, Charlie, lad, that's a fine job you're making of my boots! I'll bring you another half-dozen pairs when I come again.'

'When will you come?' The boy raised his white face wistfully. 'Soon?'

'Aye, lad, as soon as I can.' He rested his hand on his shoulder for a moment with a gentle pressure. 'Look after your mother!'

'I will that, Mr. Ravensbourne!' The lad smiled, reassured, they gripped hands, and then William was in the hall, had kissed Amy, given a pat to Rip and a bow to Catherine, and almost before they knew it he was in the cab again and on his way to the station.

'He's a fine man, that one,' said Mrs. Huggins as she closed the door behind him and led the way upstairs. 'Did you hear the way he spoke to my Charlie? He never lets him think for a moment that he's not able to look after his mother, though the accident at the mills that killed his father made him a helpless cripple for life. It was Mr. William who bought this house for us, and had our Charlie taught the trade of shoemaking, and that's not all he's done. There's much more I could tell you — aye, and others could an' all — about the way he puts new heart into you and somehow gives you the strength to battle on . . . Eh, there's nobody like him in this world, I reckon . . . he's one in a thousand, is our Mr. William.'

And with a new and unaccustomed feeling of humility Catherine found that she could almost believe her.

16

Catherine and her small charge soon settled down in their new quarters, resuming their old happy life of pupil and teacher, and with a freedom now that they had not known before.

From the sitting-room window they could watch the pale morning sunshine on the aquamarine sea as the tide came in over the hard, dun-coloured sand, the water seeping in tiny rivulets into the brown seaweed, and directly lessons were over Amy and Rip would go flying off over the beach. Catherine followed more slowly, walking close to where the waves broke in curling white along the shore, and enjoying the lifting of the petty restrictions of Mecklinburgh Square as much as the little girl.

Only once did she hear from her employer, a short, business-like letter, in which he told her that his aunt had left Brighton for good, that the house was to be sold, and that he himself was to leave England shortly for France. He said nothing about any future arrangements he might be making for his daughter and her governess.

In the middle of September they had an unexpected visitor in the person of Bella, who had returned to Brighton with Mrs. Trantam at the start of its fashionable season, to prepare for her wedding at the beginning of October. She wrote to Catherine saying how astonished they had been to find Number Five empty and up for sale, and more surprised still to receive her letter with her address in Worthing.

Aunt Sarah's housekeeper tells me that Mon Repos is a boarding house on the sea front, she wrote indignantly. *It seems extraordinary that Mr. Ravensbourne should consider such a house suitable for a Miss Whittingham—whatever he may think is fitting for his daughter! And apropos of that, I'm coming to see you on Friday, Kate, because I want to talk to you on an important private matter.*

Yet when she arrived on Friday morning the private matter did not seem to be important enough to be embarked on right away, and she was forced to admit that the view from their rooms was very pleasant, and that the public rooms that she had glimpsed as they entered the house looked almost good enough for a hotel. She was prettier than ever and even more fashionably dressed than Lady Ulsborne, and her conversation was mostly about Anthony and the wedding, and how disappointed they would be if Catherine did not come to it.

'I'm being married at the Parish Church,' she added, 'and the wedding breakfast is to be at Aunt Sarah's house, so that there will be no excuse. I've set my heart on you being my chief bridesmaid, Kate!' There followed an energetic description of the bridesmaids' dresses, which were to be of yellow chiffon, with brown velvet picture hats. 'Their bouquets are to be bronze and yellow chrysanthemums,' she added.

'Very pretty,' Catherine smiled at her affectionately. 'But I think Dulcie would make a much better chief bridesmaid than I would, darling!' It did not escape her that her sister looked relieved, while declaring loudly that she would not hear of it.

'All our friends will be there,' she protested. 'It will look so strange if my only sister isn't a bridesmaid!'

'But you have already told them that I am staying with friends, haven't you?' said Catherine quietly.

'Well, yes.' Bella frowned, and then her brow cleared a little. 'Of course I *could* say that the friend you were staying with had been taken seriously ill, I suppose?'

Catherine said she thought that would be an excellent idea, and waited for more confidences, but none came until after Mrs. Huggins's delicious lunch was finished and they walked across the road in the sunshine to the shore.

It was a lovely day, and the sea was like a length of grey silk: the waves gave a gentle rustle as they ran into the shore, and out at sea the smudge of smoke from a passing Channel steamer melted into the blue mists of the sky. While Rip and his mistress went off for their usual race along the sands the two sisters found a groyne, green with weed and water, that threw a sheltering shadow over the beach. Here Catherine spread the rug that she had brought and they sat down, and after a moment or two of silence Bella burst out: 'It's no good. I've got to ask you sooner or later, and it might as well be now. Kate, do you know that your employer is thinking of buying Grey Ladies?'

'What!' Catherine's astonishment was so unaffected that there could be no doubt that it was genuine.

'I was sure you didn't know!' Bella was relieved. 'I told them that you'd have written to tell me first . . .'

'But why *should* Mr. Ravensbourne buy Grey Ladies?'

'I don't know. I thought that perhaps you might have put it into his mind.'

'I?' Catherine could not help laughing. 'My darling Bella, Mr. Ravensbourne doesn't ask my advice about the houses he buys, and I certainly wouldn't presume to offer it unasked! I know nothing about his activities, and the only letter I have had from him since we have been here has been concerned solely with business matters.'

Bella frowned, her pretty face still troubled, and then she said hesitatingly, 'Then when you see him again . . . or have to write to him about anything . . . will you try to dissuade him from buying our old home?'

Catherine was about to say that it was none of her business when she happened to see her sister's face and the truth dawned on her.

'Why don't you want him to buy it?' she asked quietly.

'Well . . .' Bella flushed and floundered. 'It isn't that I wouldn't love to have you near me, Kate, and living in Grey Ladies again . . . if only it could happen in some other way!'

'You mean you wouldn't like to have me there in the humble role of governess to Mr. Ravensbourne's daughter?'

Bella glanced at her quickly. 'N-no . . . well, of course some of our friends would raise their eyebrows, but that wouldn't affect me . . . at least, not much. I'm putting this so badly that I don't wonder you are cross, but don't be, Kate, because I don't mean to be unkind. I love you too much . . . I truly do!'

'I know that, darling!' Catherine put her hand on Bella's. 'And I'm not cross. Go on with what there is to be said . . . Let me hear it all.'

'Very well. There are some friends of Anthony's, Peter and Maisie Crockford, and they want to buy Grey Ladies, and Peter is such fun, and Maisie is one of my best friends, and we are so fond of them . . . it would be the greatest fun to have them at Grey Ladies. But if this Ravensbourne creature buys the place nobody will call or take the slightest notice of him, because he's only a tradesman, you know . . . and you could be on the other side of the world for what I should see of you . . .' She faltered to a stop.

'And are the Crockfords your only reason for not wanting Mr. Ravensbourne to be there?' asked Catherine.

'Well, no . . . there is another reason, but I scarcely dare tell you that, Kate, because I don't think even you would understand.'

'Let me try, at all events!' Catherine glanced at her sister and saw the tears standing in her eyes. 'Come, Bella, you aren't afraid of me, surely, after only six months apart!'

'No, of course not, but I don't want to hurt your feelings.'

'Suppose we risk that? My feelings have grown pretty tough during the past year—they've been transplanted into some very cold soils and survived.'

'Well, then, it's Anthony,' said Bella miserably. 'He was so much in love with you. I think he still doesn't love me as much as he did you! And if you were to be near us, and in a position where he could pity you, perhaps be angry on your account . . . you know how chivalrous he is . . .' She caught her breath and Catherine took her up gently:

'You think he might forget his new love in remembering the old? Oh, my darling, silly little Bella, as if that were possible! But I know what you mean, and I promise you that if the chance comes my way I will do my best to talk Mr. Ravensbourne out of buying Grey Ladies.'

Bella gave a deep sigh of satisfaction. 'I knew I could depend on you, Kate!' The sparkle came back to her eyes and the tears dried in an instant. 'We met Lady Ulsborne in London when we were there for the Jubilee, and she said she thought you had a very good influence over him.'

'I am much obliged to her, but I feel bound to disagree,' said Catherine drily. 'From what little I have seen of him I should say that nobody has had any influence over Mr. Ravensbourne for a very long time.'

But after her sister had gone back to Brighton and Amy was in bed that night, she sat down and tried to compose a letter to her employer on the subject of Grey Ladies. It was not easy to say what she wanted, however, and after half a dozen attempts that sounded presumptuous and interfering she gave it up, and simply made a request that he would call on them the next time he was in Brighton, as there was some urgent business she would like to discuss with him.

He came a week later. She was on the pier with Amy and Rip when the child's sharp eyes saw him on the parade, striding purposefully along against the background of private houses and boarding houses that formed the sea-front of the peaceful little town, searching for them as he came, and she raced to him as fast as she could, shouting his name.

He saw her at the same moment and came to the pier entrance and caught her up in his arms as she came through the turnstile with an energy and affection that was strangely revealing to Catherine, making her aware of a small pang that could have been jealousy. It was obvious that Ravensbourne and his daughter had been discovering an increasing pleasure in each other's company while she had been busy with poor Edith, and although she was glad of it for Amy's sake, she could not help feeling pushed aside. They waited for her to join them, Amy hanging on to her father's hand and chattering about Rip and longing to show off his paces.

'Eh, he's a good dog, is Rip,' he agreed, as Catherine came through the turnstile and the three of them began to walk down the parade towards Mon Repos. 'I paid a lot of money for him, but he's worth it. He comes from good stock and he's well bred and good-tempered.' And then as Amy let go of his hand and raced off with her new possession he turned to Catherine with a smile. 'She looks bonny,' he said. 'And you look better for your stay here too, Miss Whittingham. There's some colour in your face now, and a new sparkle in your eyes.'

She thanked him quietly and he went on: 'And now will you please tell me what this urgent and important business may be? I set off directly I read your letter, which was waiting for me in Yorkshire when I got back from France the day before yesterday. I cannot imagine what it can be, unless you are thinking of getting married?'

'Certainly not!' She was so indignant that he chuckled.

'Stranger things have happened!'

'It's nothing to do with me. At least, in a way I suppose it is . . .' She found it hard to go on under the amusement in his face and then she blurted out, 'My sister tells me that you are thinking of buying Grey Ladies?'

'Your old home,' he said gravely. 'Well, I'll admit that I have considered it. Amy was so enthusiastic about it in July. According to her, Grey Ladies was the only house in Britain where every joy and comfort were to be found. The gardens were larger and more beautiful than those at Buckingham Palace, there were bees that made their honey in the attics, and owls that came into the house in the night to catch the mice . . . I was so intrigued by what I heard that I felt I must go and inspect this singular Garden of Eden for myself.'

She flushed a little at his dry tone and he went on: 'Forgive me for saying that I did not think much of it. It's a great, family mansion, over large for one little girl and her governess, even if they were to be waited on by an army of servants. It has a wilderness of gardens too, quite run to seed, and although I have no doubt that gardeners could be found to put it right, I did not feel that I should ever feel at home in the place. The countryside seems to be lavishly endowed with other equally large mansions, and I wondered if a blunt Yorkshireman like myself would be welcomed into any of them. I have had some experience, you see, in these matters.' His tone was ironical. 'But what is the urgency in all this, Miss Whittingham? As far as I know the place is still for sale, and if I heard tomorrow that it had been sold to someone else, I should not break my heart.'

'I am glad of that.' Her voice was so warm with relief that he glanced at her quizzically.

'Don't you want to be near your sister? I understood that she is to marry Sir Anthony Trantam this autumn.'

'Yes, she is, and it isn't because I don't want to be near her, but because—' She broke off. 'I can't explain.'

He frowned. 'Is it your sister who does not wish to have you for a neighbour? I think by the flush on your face that I may have hit the mark there?'

'Mr. Ravensbourne, you mustn't blame Bella. It's not her fault.' Catherine looked steadily out to sea, wishing that he would not watch her face so intently. 'Not so very long ago Anthony thought himself in love with me, and poor Bella is afraid—though, mind you, she has no need to be afraid, because she is much prettier than I am, and such a sweet, trusting little creature that I know he must adore her . . .'

'But having given up a . . . pearl of price . . . for such a sweet, trusting little creature, your sister has the good sense to fear that he might turn towards the pearl again if it were placed within his reach?' William's voice was unexpectedly gentle.

She hastened to disclaim all pretensions to Anthony's affections. 'It was only because we grew up together that he ever thought of marrying me. He relied on me too much . . . everybody said so. It is much better for him to have to play the part of protector now—' She broke off, angry because tears had forced their way into her eyes.

'Why did you refuse him?' asked William Ravensbourne. 'It would seem to be a match that would have solved most of your problems.'

'I didn't love him . . . at least, not enough.'

He asked no more questions. He said with some abruptness: 'You were right if you felt like that about him. In marriage affection is not enough.'

He left Worthing that evening, and a few days later Catherine had a brief letter from him in which he said that the house they had been discussing had been bought by some friend of Sir Anthony Trantam. The news, which should have been encouraging, did nothing but depress Catherine.

Now that Grey Ladies was lost to her she found herself wishing, most unreasonably, that she had encouraged her employer to buy it. It was a poor consolation to know that Mr Ravensbourne would not be likely to allow himself to be persuaded to do anything that he did not wish to do, and that the last person he would come to for advice would be his daughter's governess.

* * *

The invitation to Bella's wedding came, and Catherine

having refused it, left it to Bella to explain her absence to their friends. She fancied that her sister would be equal to the occasion, however. Bella's imagination had always been a fertile one and her powers of invention seldom failed her. Moreover, she would be the first to realize how much wiser it would be for Catherine not to be there to cast a shadow over her wedding-day.

Catherine had no wish to meet Anthony again in the role of happy bridegroom. Their old, happy, brother-and-sisterly comradeship had been brought to an abrupt end when he asked her to marry him, and although she did not doubt that he had loved her then, she was not quite sure that he might not still love her with a depth that he would not be able to give to her sister. She felt these fears to be almost justified when she had no word from him, and a far too ready acceptance of the situation from Bella.

She sent Bella their mother's diamonds as her wedding-present and tried to find comfort in the peaceful pattern that her life was shaping with little Amy, and even this was shattered by William Ravensbourne when he returned to Brighton in October for a day or two while he was arranging for the sale of his aunt's furniture there. The house was already sold, but business matters had to be settled and household effects to be gone through because Mrs. Ravensbourne would not keep anything that could remind her of Edith.

One afternoon he came out to see his daughter and had tea with them in their pleasant sitting-room. The sea was grey that afternoon as it rolled into the shore covering the sands, the wind was blowing cold and the sunshine pale, but only Catherine had time to observe it from their window. Amy's hand was holding fast to her father's, and her whole attention was given to him: it seemed to Catherine that here again she was not needed any more. Amy as well as Bella had found a happiness that was perfectly able to exist without her.

Before he left William Ravensbourne picked up a photograph that stood on the writing table that she was using for a desk, and asked if it was of her aunt.

'Yes.' She took up another that stood opposite it. 'And this was my father.'

He had little interest in the General, however, and beyond remarking that he was a handsome man and that she was like him, he scarcely glanced at it, nor at the lovely new one of Bella in her wedding-dress that was between the two. He asked for

Miss Abbott's address and said that he might go and see her before he went back to Yorkshire. He said nothing about how his search for a house was progressing and Catherine did not ask him, reminding herself severely that it was none of her business. The next day, however, she wrote to her aunt to prepare her for the possible visit.

I know he has a blunt, unprepossessing manner, she wrote *but you must not go by appearances. He certainly is not the monster I first took him for, I had a very wrong impression of him.*

She waited with some anxiety for Miss Abbott's reply, and although when it came she learned that the visit had been made, her aunt was disappointingly guarded in what she said of William Ravensbourne.

I am afraid your uncle did not like him very much, she said *His downright way displeased him, I think. I find that in a suburban society people are over-anxious to retain their status of ladies and gentlemen. There is an unkind snobbery in their attitude towards strangers that can be very trying.*

So her Uncle Josiah had not considered Mr. Ravensbourne to be a gentleman ... Catherine felt herself growing warm with indignation and wrote again to ask Miss Abbott's opinion of him, but her aunt did not reply, and in the meantime trouble at the mills kept her employer bound to Yorkshire. Through Mrs. Huggins Catherine learned that the business that kept him was something to do with a plan he had for sharing profits with the workers in the Ravensbourne mills.

'There's others have had the same idea before him,' she told her ominously. 'Some have been successful, others have gone bankrupt. I don't rightly know the ins and outs of it myself but from what I hear William Ravensbourne intends going on with it in the face of opposition from his partners. I hope he don't lose his brass, all the same. He don't deserve that, don' Mr. William.'

Listening to her stories of the mills during those long evenings after Amy was in bed, Catherine felt a new respect for William Ravensbourne and for those who worked for him. The picture Eliza built up for her was of a stocky, sturdy race of people, as able to build up a big business out of nothing as they were to throw it away, according to some, in a dream of the future.

She was unprepared for the letter that arrived on the first of November telling her to be ready to leave Mon Repos at the end of the week, as Amy's new home was ready and waiting for her.

Catherine answered Amy's eager questions at random as she packed: she was as ignorant as the child could be of their destination, and Mrs. Huggins, to whom they both applied for information, seemed to be as much in the dark as they were. Maybe the house was in London, she said, or maybe it was in Yorkshire. They must wait and see.

'Mr. William likes to surprise folk,' she added with a grim smile.

Their trunks were packed and corded and down in the hall on the appointed day, and early in the morning a private carriage drew up in front of the house, driven by a coachman who touched his hat in greeting to Mrs. Huggins, and accompanied by a groom at whom Amy stared as if she could not believe her eyes before giving a shriek of delight and flinging herself upon him.

'Albert!' she cried. 'Oh, Albert, how nice to see you again!' And then some of the joy went out of her face as she asked, 'Have you come to take me back to Brighton?'

'No, that I haven't, Miss Amy!' said Albert, grinning all over his face. 'It's Mr. Ravensbourne what employs me now, not your auntie, and he's here too.' And with that he opened the carriage door and William Ravensbourne got out and ran up the steps, stopping to embrace Amy swiftly before going on into the house.

'Are you ready?' he asked Catherine impatiently. 'Miss Whittingham, are those all the cases you have? Are there no more? . . . And where is Eliza?' More animated than she had ever seen him, Catherine's employer sought out Eliza in the kitchen, gave her what he owed her and said he could never pay her for her kindness because it wasn't included in her bills and couldn't be rightly rewarded anyway, and then he found Charlie and settled with him for his last pairs of boots, which he sent by Albert after the luggage. By this time Amy's excitement was getting the better of her, and Rip's lead was becoming twisted first round Eliza and then Catherine and then herself, until her father summoned Albert firmly and told him to take her and Rip down to the carriage and to put them both inside it and out of everyone's way.

A pony-cart, led by a stable-boy, was drawn up behind the carriage and in this Albert helped the lad to stow away the cases, until they were all there, and when the last package was stowed away the stable-boy got up beside them, the pony's reins in his hands, while the coachman waited for Albert to close the carriage door.

Mrs. Huggins kissed Amy goodbye and shook hands with Catherine and said mysteriously that she did not doubt she'd see them again before long. Charlie waved from his window, the door of the carriage was finally shut upon them, and they moved off towards the railway station, still without a word being spoken as to their destination.

And then, just as they were approaching the station road, they turned off into a wide avenue, where large houses stood back in pleasant gardens, and half-way down this road a pair of gates stood open as if someone was expected there.

The driveway led to a gravel sweep in front of a house that was long and low and homely, with a verandah running round it and a balcony above. In the pale sunshine of the November morning they could see that the house had been freshly painted, and the curtains hanging beside the long, polished windows were as fresh and as new as the paint.

They turned in at the open gates and stopped in the drive before the front door: Albert leaped down to help them out, and Catherine caught sight of somebody standing at one of the downstairs windows, anxiously watching for them. Somebody who scarcely waited for the old butler to open the door, but was there behind him, her arms wide open to receive her beloved niece, and including in their embrace the child whose home it was to be.

'Aunt Emily!' Catherine's arms went round the little lady's neck in a hug that nearly throttled her. 'Oh, Aunt Emily, have you been here in Worthing all the time and we didn't know?' She held out a hand to the butler. 'And Grindall . . . dear old Grindall! Where did Aunt Emily find you, and how did she persuade you to leave home?'

There was somebody else standing in the hall behind Grindall though, someone in a new, neat uniform, because she was promoted now to parlourmaid, and with shining hair under a smart new cap, that nevertheless got knocked to one side in the old way when Amy rushed into her arms, and there was all the old tenderness in Maggie's voice when she called her her 'little love'.

But when all the exclamations and delight and admiration came to a halt, because nobody could think of anything more to say that would express their feelings, it was William Ravensbourne who had the last word.

He had been a silent spectator in the doorway, and now, as the carriage moved off empty to the stables, he sought out his daughter, and stooping he put his hands on her shoulders and smiled down into her delighted little face.

'Well,' he said gruffly, 'does it please you, then, so much? It's eight years late, I'm afraid, and it's been a long time coming . . . but it's all yours at last . . . Welcome home, my darling. Welcome home!'

*   *   *

Lunch was served to them in a pleasant dining-room looking out on the garden at the back, where an old cedar tree stooped to brush the velvety surface of the lawn, and over the meal William told them how he had considered the problem of his future home.

'I am no longer wanted so often in Yorkshire,' he said. 'I have two brothers who manage for me there, and I have always been head salesman for the mills, travelling between England and the Continent and even to America, with samples of our cloth. For a long time now I have wanted an unassuming and modest house of my own to come to, easy to reach, and yet with the fresh air of the country in it. Worthing is a charming little town, and the houses I saw as I drove to and from the station during the summer struck me as being very much what was needed for Amy's new home. Quite by chance I heard that this house was for sale, I came to look at it, and decided on the spot that I need look no further. It is, as you see, not ostentatious or imposing, but roomy and comfortable, and the garden is large enough for a little girl and a small dog to play in without going outside the garden wall on a lazy summer afternoon. The stabling, too, is sufficient for a couple of carriages, a pony-cart and half a dozen horses—I like driving a four-in-hand—and there is a piece of land behind it for a tennis court. Having bought the house I had only to approach Miss Abbott and persuade her to come here as your companion and chaperon, Miss Whittingham, and I may add,' he went on with a smiling glance at Miss Abbott who was settled serenely at the foot of the table, 'that she did not need a lot of persuasion! And the deed was done.'

If he had made any business arrangement with Miss Abbott it was never mentioned then or later: he deferred to her respectfully and affectionately as he would to the mistress of the house, and it was a role that fitted her like a glove. Catherine was astonished to discover how easily her aunt had slipped into the position that was waiting for her there, and she wondered what Ravensbourne had said or done that had given her such an air of authority, because in the old days she had depended on her nieces for everything, and it had been the elder Miss Whittingham who had been mistress of Grey Ladies.

But William Ravensbourne had simply told her how much they all wanted her to look after them, and how much he personally needed a wise and sensible woman to manage his house, and in that moment he had restored the pride that her odious brother-in-law had done his best to destroy throughout a long and tedious summer, and gave her a feeling of being indispensable that put inches on to her stature.

After the meal he left her to take them over the rest of the house, and when they reached the big, airy room that was to be Amy's schoolroom Catherine found that all the pictures from the Brighton attic had been carefully reframed, and most of the books repaired, and where repair was not possible new editions replaced those that had been destroyed.

Miss Abbott opened the lid of the cottage piano in the corner.

'There is a grand piano in the drawing-room downstairs,' she said, 'but we thought this would be good enough for Amy to learn on. Mr. Ravensbourne furnished his own rooms himself but he left the choice of everything else to me.' Her eyes sparkled. 'I cannot tell you when I have enjoyed anything so much: to be able to go into those big London stores and order anything that took my fancy, regardless of cost! And then there was the speed at which all my orders were carried out—the name of Ravensbourne seemed to work like a magic charm. An army of workmen arrived down here and set to with a will, painting and papering, and hanging curtains and laying carpets. You never saw anything like it. I stayed in rooms that Mrs. Huggins found for me near the station while it was all being done, and I was only afraid that I might run into you one day in the town and give the game away! I did see you once, Kate, and I turned and ran for my life. Mr. Ravensbourne insisted that it was to be a complete surprise.'

Amy was busy on her knees by the bookshelf, examining all her old favourites there, and Miss Abbott put her hand on her niece's arm and dropped her voice. 'I feel I ought to tell you, Kate, that you were quite wrong in your opinion of Mr. Ravensbourne. He is one of the kindest and most generous of men, and all through these last few weeks it has seemed that he could not do enough for little Amy ... or for you.' She looked at Catherine reproachfully and her niece coloured up and said that she had revised her first opinion of Amy's father considerably.

'And I should hope so too!' said her aunt. 'From the letters I had from you during the spring and early summer one would have thought him to be a heartless brute.'

Catherine looked into the fire and saw a curling ash in an empty grate and a name, bold and brazen, in black on grey, and she said humbly, 'I assure you, Aunt Em, that I haven't thought him heartless for a long time now.'

'I am glad to hear it.' Miss Abbott was still inclined to be indignant, and then she broke off to laugh at Rip, who had discovered the new basket in front of the schoolroom fire and curled himself up in it. 'Look!' she cried. 'Look, Amy love! ... Even little Rip knows that he is home!'

17

Once more Catherine and Amy settled down, this time in a house from which there was no fear that Amy would be ejected, or pushed into the background until somebody found time to remember her.

Everything had been done to ensure the child's comfort and happiness, and on the evenings of the days when her father was at home he would push aside his books and business papers to devote his time to her. And the closer that he and his daughter drew to each other, the more it seemed that Catherine was left outside. Once more a magic circle was closed and complete without her, as Bella's gay little group had been in Brighton in the spring, and although she was not ungenerous enough to grudge Amy or Miss Abbott the happiness they had found in William Ravensbourne's house, she could not shake off the depression that settled over her spirits.

From the depth of Amy's delight in her father she was able now to realize that the love she had held out to the child could have only been a pale shadow of what she had needed, although, starved as she was for affection, she had clung to it for want of something better. There were times when she thought that mutual loneliness had played a big part in drawing them together in the garret schoolroom, and her restless spirit questioned it after all Anthony had not been right when he said that children soon forget.

Her own treatment of Anthony was not the only matter for self-reproach. Every morning when Miss Abbott bustled off to interview her housekeeper, in her hand a bundle of household books and a little basket of keys that were quite useless because nothing was ever locked away in that open-handed house, Catherine thought of the years when her aunt had been affectionately tolerated at Grey Ladies. She remembered the slights that had been offered to the gentle little lady, the snubs that had been openly administered by the General, and the patronage of his friends, and the countless occasions when her quiet attempts at conversation had been contemptuously brushed aside or cut short, not only by her brother-in-law but by his daughters.

Remorse for the part she had played in the past made her careful not to encroach now by a hair's breadth on her authority, and she learned to treat her with deference because of the respect that William Ravensbourne showed her.

'Miss Abbott,' he said one morning just before the carriage took him to the station, 'I shall be back from Yorkshire next Tuesday, and I shall be bringing with me some friends who will be dining here and staying the night. Will you arrange this for me please, in your usual admirable fashion?'

'Certainly, Mr. Ravensbourne.' Miss Abbott took the news with a calm that she would never have shown at Grey Ladies. 'How many will there be?'

Five he told her—himself and four guests. 'But dinner for six, of course . . . unless Miss Whittingham likes to join us?'

Catherine said hastily that she would spend the evening finishing some needlework in the schoolroom, and when on the following Tuesday evening she heard Miss Abbott's voice talking composedly and cheerfully as she went through the hall to the dining-room on the arm of the most important guest, she wondered why they had never heard that voice properly at Grey Ladies.

After that, on the days when Ravensbourne was at home, she withdrew still more into her shell, slipping away to the schoolroom and leaving him alone with Amy and Miss Abbott, and he did not seem to notice her absence. His greeting over breakfast in the morning was brief and cheerful, and he appeared to have far more interest in how Rip had passed his night than if anyone else in the house had slept.

And then, one crisp December morning, while Amy was having a riding lesson in the lanes round Broadwater, and Miss Abbott was at the vicarage, attached to the church on the corner, attending a Ladies' Committee Meeting for the next bazaar, Lady Ulsborne was shown into the schoolroom where Catherine was sitting alone with Rip.

'My dearest Kate!' Helen kissed her with all the old warmth, bringing into the room a scent of furs and violets. 'Dick is helping the poor Ansteys with this stupid election at Burrington, and as we have politics for breakfast, lunch and dinner, and Burrington is only a few miles away, I borrowed Lady Anstey's little brougham and fled to you for comfort. I told her I wanted to see Will's new house, but really, of course, I wanted to see you!' She looked round her at the schoolroom. 'This is charming. I congratulate you on your taste, my love! The whole house is what I would have expected of you.'

'But I had nothing to do with it!' cried Catherine. 'It was all done long before I set eyes on it.'

Lady Ulsborne shook her head. 'You have been very clever, but there's no need to be so modest about it. You have your aunt, Miss Abbott, living here, haven't you? So wise of you! One can't be too careful.'

'I don't know what you mean.' Catherine's eyes met hers

steadily. 'But if it is what I think I may as well tell you at once that Mr. Ravensbourne has no interest in me beyond regarding me as Amy's governess.'

'You surprise me!' Helen laughed and changed the subject. 'Did you ever find poor Mary's sandalwood box?'

'Yes. Edith had it.'

'I thought she might. She was deep, was Edith, and not a very pleasant sort of person. She hated poor Mary.'

Catherine was prompted to remark that perhaps it was not without reason.

Helen shrugged her shoulders. 'Oh well,' she said evasively, 'of course Mary used to tease her, but then Edith was a very easy person to tease.'

Catherine was silent, thinking of poor, unhappy Edith, and then she asked, 'Helen, have you any idea what could have been in the letter in the sandalwood box?'

'Why no . . . of course not. Why do you ask?'

'Only because of the effect it had on Mr. Ravensbourne when he read it,' said Catherine simply.

'Will read it?'

'Yes. I have been trying to think what your sister could have said to hurt him so terribly.'

The laughter died out of Helen Ulsborne's face. 'Perhaps she told the truth,' she said. 'He may not have guessed it before, but that was his fault, you know. He would put her on a pedestal, and even when she did a bolt with Tempest he insisted it wasn't her wish, that she had been persuaded against her better self, and so on . . . Poor Will.'

'I'm afraid I don't understand.' Catherine was perplexed. 'What *was* the truth about your sister and Captain Tempest?'

Helen caressed Rip's sleek head. 'That she was Tempest's mistress long before she married Will,' she said calmly.

'Oh no!' Catherine stared at her in horror. 'I don't believe it . . .'

'My dear little innocent, it happens to be true.' There was a trace of impatience in Lady Ulsborne's musical voice. 'It's so boring to pretend that these things don't happen. Of course they happen, when two people are as much in love as Mary and Tempest, and have no money to marry on. If Will was hurt I'm sorry, but he ought to have guessed it long ago, and I daresay it didn't break his heart. And if it did, no doubt somebody will be ready to mend it for him in due course. A man as